MISSILE OF DEATH

It was painted a very bright red. An odd color for anything in space, for red was the sign of danger. It was only fifty feet beyond their port, drifting . . . silent, mysterious, ominous. As it slowly revolved, a black pattern on a white background came into view, a pattern only too terrifyingly familiar. Then, there was no longer any reason for doubt. For on the side of the approaching missile they saw a skull and crossbones . . .

Other SIGNET Titles You Will Want to Read

ARTHUR C. CLARKE

ISLANDS IN THE SKY

A SIGNET BOOK from
NEW AMERICAN LIBRARY
TIMES MIRROR

For Ian
*From an Elizabethan
to a Georgian*

*Published as a SIGNET BOOK
By arrangement with Holt, Rinehart and Winston, Inc.*

SEVENTH PRINTING
EIGHTH PRINTING
NINTH PRINTING
TENTH PRINTING
ELEVENTH PRINTING
TWELFTH PRINTING
THIRTEENTH PRINTING
FOURTEENTH PRINTING
FIFTEENTH PRINTING
SIXTEENTH PRINTING

 SIGNET TRADEMARK REG. U.S. PAT. OFF. AND FOREIGN COUNTRIES
REGISTERED TRADEMARK—MARCA REGISTRADA
HECHO EN CHICAGO, U.S.A.

SIGNET, SIGNET CLASSICS, SIGNETTE, MENTOR AND PLUME BOOKS
*are published by The New American Library, Inc.,
1301 Avenue of the Americas, New York, New York 10019*

FIRST PRINTING, MARCH, 1960

PRINTED IN THE UNITED STATES OF AMERICA

CONTENTS

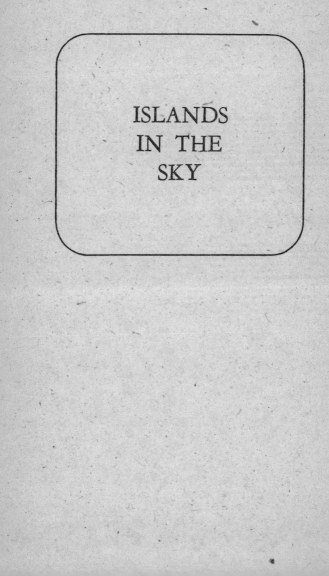

ISLANDS
IN THE
SKY

1 JACKPOT TO SPACE

◆◆◆

IT WAS UNCLE JIM who'd said, "Whatever happens, Roy, don't *worry* about it. Just relax and enjoy yourself." I remembered those words as I followed the other competitors into the big studio, and I don't think I felt particularly nervous. After all, however badly I wanted the prize, it was only a game.

The audience was already in its place, talking and fidgeting and waiting for the program to begin. It gave a little cheer as we walked up on to the stage and took our seats. I had a quick look at the five other competitors, and was a bit disappointed. Each of them looked quite sure that *he* was going to win.

There was another cheer from the audience as Elmer Schmitz, the Quiz Master, came into the studio. I'd met him before, of course, in the semifinals, and I expect you've seen him often enough on TV. He gave us some last minute instructions, moved to his place under the spotlights, and signaled to the cameras. There was a sudden hush as the red light came on. From where I was sitting I could see Elmer adjusting his smile.

"Good evening, folks! This is Elmer Schmitz, presenting to you the finalists in our Aviation Quiz Program, brought to you by arrangement with World Airways, Incorporated. The six young men we have here tonight . . ."

But I guess it wouldn't be very modest to repeat the things he said about us. It all added up to the fact that we knew a lot about everything that flew—in the air and outside it—and had beaten about five thousand other members of the Junior Rocket Club in a series of nationwide contests. Tonight would be the final elimination tests to select the winner.

It started easily enough, on the lines of earlier rounds. Elmer fired off a question at each of us in turn, and we had twenty seconds in which to answer. Mine was pretty easy; he wanted to know the altitude record for a pure jet. Everyone else got his answer right too. I think those first questions were just to give us confidence.

Then it got tougher. We couldn't see our scores, which were being flashed up on a screen facing the audience, but you could tell when you'd given the right answer by the noise they made. I forgot to say that you *lost* a point when you gave the wrong reply. That was to prevent guessing. If you didn't know, it was best to say nothing at all.

As far as I could tell, I'd made only one mistake, but there was a kid from New Washington who I thought hadn't made any—though I couldn't be sure of this, because it was difficult to keep track of the others while you were wondering what Elmer had coming up for you. I was feeling rather gloomy, when suddenly the lights dimmed and a hidden movie projector went into action.

"Now," said Elmer, "the last round! You'll each see some kind of aircraft or rocket for *one second* and in that time you must identify it. Ready?"

A second sounds awfully short, but it isn't really. You can grasp a great deal in that time, enough to recognize anything you know really well. But some of the machines they showed us went back over a hundred years. One or two even had propellors! This was lucky for me: I'd always been interested in the history of flying and could spot some of those antiques. That was where the boy from New Washington fell down badly. They gave him a picture of the original Wright biplane, which you can see in the Smithsonian any day, and he didn't know it. Afterward he said he was interested only in rockets, and that the test wasn't fair. But I thought it served him right.

They gave me the Dornier DO-X and a B-52, and I knew them both. So I wasn't really surprised when Elmer called out my name as soon as the lights went up. Still, it was a proud moment as I walked over to him, with the cameras following me and the audience clapping in the background.

"Congratulations, Roy!" said Elmer heartily, shaking my hand. "Almost a perfect score. You missed only one question. I have great pleasure in announcing you as the winner of this World Airways Contest. As you know, the prize is a trip, all expenses paid, to any place in the world. We're all interested to hear your choice. What is it going to be? You can go anywhere you like between the North and South Poles!"

My lips went kind of dry. Though I'd made all my plans weeks ago, it was different now that the time had actually come. I felt awfully lonely in that huge studio, with everyone around me so quiet and waiting for what I was going to say. My voice sounded a long way off when I answered.

"I want to go to the Inner Station."

Elmer looked puzzled, surprised and annoyed all at once. There was a sort of rustle from the audience, and I heard someone give a little laugh. Perhaps that made Elmer decide to be funny too.

"Ha, ha, very amusing, Roy! But the prize is anywhere on earth. You must stick to the rules, you know!"

I could tell he was laughing at me, and that made me mad. So I came back with: "I've read the rules very carefully. And they *don't* say 'on earth.' They say, 'To any part *of* the earth.' There's a big difference."

Elmer was smart. He knew there was trouble brewing, for his grin faded out at once, and he looked anxiously at the TV cameras.

"Go on," he said.

I cleared my throat.

"In 2054," I continued, "the United States, like all the other members of the Atlantic Federation, signed the Tycho Convention, which decided how far into space any planet's legal rights extended. Under that Convention, the Inner Station is part of earth, because it's inside the thousand kilometer limit."

Elmer gave me a most peculiar look. Then he relaxed a little and said, "Tell me, Roy, is your dad an attorney?"

I shook my head. "No, he isn't."

Of course I might have added, "But my Uncle Jim is." I decided not to; there was going to be enough trouble anyway.

Elmer made a few attempts to make me change my mind, but there was nothing doing. Time was running out, and the audience was on my side. Finally he gave up and said with a laugh:

"Well, you're a very determined young man. You've won the prize, anyway, and it looks as if the legal eagles take over from here. I hope there's something left for you when they've finished wrangling!"

I rather hoped so too!

Of course, Elmer was right in thinking I'd not worked all this out by myself. Uncle Jim, who's counselor for a big atomic energy combine, had spotted the opportunity soon after I'd entered the contest. He'd told me what to say and had promised that World Airways couldn't wriggle out of it. Even if they could, so many people had seen me on the air that it would be very bad publicity for them if they tried. "Just stick to your guns, Roy," he'd said, "and don't agree to anything until you've talked it over with me."

Mom and Pop were pretty mad about the whole business. They'd been watching, and as soon as I started bargaining they knew what had happened. Pop rang up Uncle Jim at once and gave him a piece of his mind (I heard about it afterward), but it was too late for them to stop me.

You see, I'd been crazy to go out into space for as long as I can remember. I was sixteen when all this happened, and rather big for my age. I'd read everything I could get hold of about aviation and astronautics, seen all the movies and telecasts from space, and made up my mind that someday *I* was going to look back and watch the earth shrinking behind me. I'd made models of famous spaceships, and put rocket units in some of them until the neighbors raised a fuss. In my room I have hundreds of photographs, not only of most of the ships you care to name, but all the important places on the planets as well.

Mom and Pop had not minded this interest, but they thought it was something I'd grow out of. "Look at Joe Donovan," they'd say. (Joe's the chap who runs the 'copter repair depot in our district.) *"He* was going to be a Martian colonist when he was your age. Earth wasn't good enough for him! Well, he's never been as far as the moon, and I don't suppose he ever will. He's quite happy here." But I wasn't so sure. I've seen Joe looking up at the sky as the outgoing rockets draw their white vapor trails through the stratosphere, and sometimes I think he'd give everything he owns to go with them.

Uncle Jim (that's Pop's brother) was the one who really understood how I felt about things. He'd been to Mars two or three times, to Venus once, and to the moon so often he couldn't count the times. He had the kind of job where people actually paid him to do these things. I'm afraid he was considered a very disturbing influence around our house.

It was about a week after I won the contest that I heard from World Airways. They were very polite, in an icy sort of way, and said that they'd agreed that the terms of the competition allowed me to go to the Inner Station. (They couldn't help adding their disappointment that I hadn't chosen to go on one of their luxury flights inside the atmosphere. Uncle Jim said what really upset them was the fact that my choice would cost at least ten times as much as they'd bargained for.) There were, however, two conditions. First, I had to get my parents' consent. Second, I would have to pass the standard medical tests for space crew.

I'll say this about Mom and Pop—though they were still pretty mad, they wouldn't stand in my way. After all, space travel was safe enough, and I was only going a few hundred miles up—scarcely any distance! So after a little argument they signed the forms and sent them off. I'm pretty sure that World Airways had hoped they'd refuse to let me go.

That left the second obstacle, the medical exam. I didn't think it was fair having to take that: from all accounts it was pretty tough, and if I failed, no one would be more pleased than World Airways.

The nearest place where I could take the tests was the Department of Space Medicine at Johns Hopkins, which meant an hour's flying in the Kansas-Washington jet and a couple of short 'copter trips at either end. Though I'd made dozens of longer journeys, I was so excited that it seemed like a new experience. In a way, of course, it was, because if everything went properly it would open up a new chapter in my life.

I'd got everything ready the night before, even though I was going to be away from home for only a few hours. It was a fine evening, so I carried my little telescope out of doors to have a look at the stars. It's not much of an instrument—just a couple of lenses in a wooden tube—but I'd made it myself and was quite proud of it. When the moon was half-full, it would show all the bigger lunar mountains, as well as Saturn's rings and the moons of Jupiter.

But tonight I was after something else, something not so easy to find. I knew its approximate orbit, because our local astronomer's club had worked out the figures for me. So I set up the telescope as carefully as I could and slowly began to sweep across the stars to the southwest, checking against the map I'd already prepared.

The search took about fifteen minutes. In the field of the telescope was a handful of stars—and something that was not a star. I could just make out a tiny oval shape, far too small to show any details. It shone brilliantly up there in the blazing sunlight outside the shadow of the earth, and it was moving even as I watched. An astronomer of a century before would have been sorely puzzled by it, for it was something new in the sky. It was Met Station Two, six thousand miles up and circling the earth four times a day. The Inner Station was too far to the south to be visible from my latitude: you had to live near the Equator to see it shining in the sky, the brightest and most swiftly moving of all the "stars."

I tried to imagine what it was like up there in that floating bubble, with the emptiness of space all around. At this very moment, the scientists aboard must be looking down at me just as I was looking up at them. I wondered what kind of life they led—and remembered that with any luck I'd soon know for myself.

The bright, tiny disk I had been watching suddenly turned orange, then red, and began to fade from sight like a dying ember. In a few seconds it had vanished completely, though the stars were still shining as brightly as ever in the field of the telescope. Met Station Two had raced into the shadow of the earth and would remain eclipsed until it emerged again, about an hour later, in the southeast. It was "night" aboard the Space Station, just as it was down here on earth. I packed up the telescope and went to bed.

East of Kansas City, where I went aboard the Washington jet, the land is flat for five hundred miles until you reach the Appalachians. A century earlier I should have been flying over millions of acres of farm land, but that had all vanished when agriculture moved out to sea at the end of the twentieth century. Now the ancient prairies were coming back, and with them the great buffalo herds that had roamed this land when the Indians were its only masters. The main industrial cities and mining centers hadn't changed much, but the smaller towns had vanished and in a few more years there would be no sign that they had ever existed.

I think I was a lot more nervous when I went up the wide marble steps of the Department of Space Medicine than when I entered the final round of the World Airways Contest. If I'd failed that, I might have had another chance later—but if the doctors said "no," then I'd never be able to go out into space.

There were two kinds of tests, the physical and the psychological. I had to do all sorts of silly things, like running on a treadmill while holding my breath, trying to hear very faint sounds in a noiseproof room, and identifying dim, colored lights. At one point they amplified my heartbeat thousands of times: it was an eerie sound and gave me the creeps, but the doctors said it was O.K.

They seemed a very friendly crowd, and after a while I got the definite impression that they were on my side and doing their best to get me through. Of course, that helped a lot and I began to think it was all good fun—almost a game, in fact.

I changed my mind after a test in which they sat me inside a box and spun it round in every possible direction. When I came out I was horribly sick and couldn't stand upright. That was the worst moment I had, because I was sure I'd failed. But it was really all right: if I *hadn't* been sick there would have been something wrong with me!

After all this they let me rest for an hour before the psychological tests. I wasn't worried much about those, as I'd met them before. There were some simple jigsaw puzzles, a few sheets of questions to be answered ("Four of the following five words have something in common. Underline them.") and some tests for quickness of eye and hand. Finally they attached a lot of wires to my head and took me into a narrow, darkened corridor with a closed door ahead of me.

"Now listen carefully, Roy," said the psychologist who'd

been doing the tests. "I'm going to leave you now, and the lights will go out. Stand here until you receive further instructions, and then do exactly what you're told. Don't worry about these wires. They will follow you when you move. O.K.?"

"Yes," I said, wondering what was going to happen next.

The lights dimmed, and for a minute I was in complete darkness. Then a very faint rectangle of red light appeared, and I knew that the door ahead of me was opening, though I couldn't hear a sound. I tried to see what was beyond the door, but the light was too dim.

I knew the wires that had been attached to my head were recording my brain impulses. So whatever happened, I would try to keep calm and collected.

A voice came out of the darkness from a hidden loud-speaker.

"Walk through the door you see ahead of you, and stop as soon as you have passed it."

I obeyed the order, though it wasn't easy to walk straight in that faint light, with a tangle of wires trailing behind me.

I never heard the door shutting, but I knew somehow that it had closed, and when I reached back with my hand I found I was standing in front of a smooth sheet of plastic. It was completely dark now; even the dim red light had gone.

It seemed a long time before anything happened. I must have been standing there in the darkness for almost ten minutes, waiting for the next order. Once or twice I whistled softly, to see if there was any echo by which I could judge the size of the room. Though I couldn't be sure, I got the impression that it was quite a large place.

Then, without any warning, the lights came on, not in a sudden flash, which would have blinded me, but in a very quick build-up that took only two or three seconds. I was able to see my surroundings perfectly, and I'm not ashamed to say that I yelled.

It was a perfectly normal room, except for one thing. There was a table with some papers lying on it, three arm-chairs, bookcases against one wall, a small desk, an ordinary TV set. The sun seemed to be shining through the window, and some curtains were waving slightly in the breeze. At the moment the lights came on, the door opened and a man walked in. He picked up a paper from the table, and flopped down in one of the chairs. He was just beginning to read when he looked up and saw me. And when I say "up," I mean it. For that's what was wrong with the room. I wasn't standing on the floor, down there with the chairs and bookcases. I was fifteen feet up in the air, scared out of my wits and flattened against the "ceiling," with no means of support and nothing within reach to catch hold of! I clawed at the smooth surface behind me, but it was as flat as glass. There was no way to stop myself from falling, and the floor looked very hard and a long way down.

2 GOOD-BY TO GRAVITY

━━

THE FALL NEVER CAME, and my moment of panic passed swiftly. The whole thing was an illusion of some kind, for the floor felt firm beneath my feet, whatever my eyes told me. I stopped clutching at the door through which I had entered, the door which my eyes tried to convince me was part of the ceiling.

Of course, it was absurdly simple! The room I seemed to be looking *down* at was really seen reflected in a large mirror immediately in front of me, a mirror at an angle of forty-five degrees to the vertical. I was actually standing in the upper part of a tall room that was "bent" horizontally through a right angle, but because of the mirror there was no way of telling this.

I went down on my hands and knees and cautiously edged my way forward. It took a lot of will power to do this, for my eyes still told me that I was crawling head-first down the side of a vertical wall. After a few feet, I came to a sudden drop and peered over the edge. There below me, really *below* me this time, was the room into which I had been looking! The man in the armchair was grinning up at me as if to say, "We gave you quite a shock, didn't we?" I could see him equally well, of course, by looking at his reflection in the mirror straight ahead of me.

The door behind me opened and the psychologist came in. He was carrying a long strip of paper in his hand, and he chuckled as he waved it at me.

"We've got all your reactions on the tape, Roy," he said. "Do you know what this test was for?"

"I think I can guess," I said, a little ruefully. "Is it to discover how I behave when gravity is wrong?"

"That's the idea. It's what we call an orientation test. In space you won't have any gravity at all, and some people are never able to get used to it. This test eliminates most of them."

I hoped it wouldn't eliminate me, and I spent a very uncomfortable half-hour waiting for the doctors to make up their minds. But I needn't have worried. As I said before, they were on my side and were just as determined to get me through as I was myself.

The New Guinea mountains, just south of the Equator and rising in places more than three miles above sea level, must once have been about the wildest and most inaccessible spots on earth. Although the helicopter had made them as easy to reach as anywhere else, it was not until the twenty-first century that they became important as the world's main springboard into space.

There are three good reasons for this. First of all, the fact that they are so near the Equator means that, because of the earth's spin, they're moving from west to east at a thousand miles an hour. That's quite a useful start for a ship on its way out to space. Their height means that all the denser layers of the atmosphere are below them, thus the air resistance is reduced and the rockets can work more efficiently. And perhaps most important of all is the fact that there are ten thousand miles of open Pacific stretching away from them to the east. You can't launch spaceships from inhabited areas, because apart from the danger if anything goes wrong, the unbelievable noise of an ascending ship would deafen everyone for miles around.

Port Goddard is on a great plateau, leveled by atomic blasting, almost two and a half miles up. There is no way to reach it by land—everything comes in by air. It is the meeting place for ships of the atmosphere and ships of space.

When I first saw it from our approaching jet, it looked like a tiny white rectangle among the mountains. Great valleys packed with tropical forests stretched as far as one could see. In some of those valleys, I was told, there are still savage tribes that no one has ever contacted. I wonder what they thought of the monsters flying above their heads and filling the sky with their roaring!

The small amount of luggage I had been allowed to take had been sent on ahead of me, and I wouldn't see it again until I reached the Inner Station. When I stepped out of the jet into the cold, clear air of Port Goddard, I already felt so far above sea level that I automatically looked up into the sky to see if I could find my destination. But I wasn't allowed time for the search. The reporters were waiting for me, and I had to go in front of the cameras again.

I haven't any idea what I said, and fortunately one of the port officials soon rescued me. There were the inevitable forms to be filled. I was weighed very carefully and given some pills to swallow (they made sure that I did, too), and then we climbed aboard a little truck that would take us out to the launching site. I was the only passenger on this trip, as the rocket on which I was traveling was really a freighter.

Most spaceships, naturally enough, have astronomical names. I was flying on the *Sirius,* and though she was one of the smaller ships, she looked impressive enough as we came up to her. She had already been raised in her supporting cradle so that her prow pointed vertically at the sky, and she seemed to be balanced on the great triangles of her wings. These would come into action only when she glided back into the atmosphere on her return to earth; at the moment they served merely as supports for the four huge fuel tanks, like giant bombs, which would be jettisoned as soon as the motors had drained them dry. These streamlined tanks were nearly as large as the ship's hull itself.

The servicing gantry was still in position, and as I stepped into the elevator I realized for the first time that I had now cut myself off from earth. A motor began to whine, and the metal walls of the *Sirius* slid swiftly past. My view of Port Goddard widened. Now I could see all the administrative buildings clustering at the edge of the plateau, the great fuel storage tanks, the strange machinery of the liquid ozone plant, the airfield with its everyday jets and helicopters. And beyond all these, quite unchanged by everything that man had done, the eternal mountains and forests.

The elevator came gently to a halt, and the gates opened on to a short gangway leading into the *Sirius*. I walked across it, through the open seals of the air lock, and the brilliant tropical sunlight gave way to the cold electric glare of the ship's control room.

The pilot was already in his seat, going through the routine checks. He swiveled round as I entered and gave me a cheerful grin.

"So you're the famous Roy Malcolm, are you? I'll try and get you to the station in one piece. Have you flown in a rocket before?"

"No," I replied.

"Then don't worry. It's not as bad as some people pretend. Make yourself comfortable in that seat, fasten the straps, and just relax. We've still got twenty minutes before take-off."

I climbed into the pneumatic couch, but it wasn't easy to relax. I don't think I was frightened, but I was certainly excited. After all these years of dreaming, I was really aboard a spaceship at last! In a few minutes, more than a hundred million horsepower would be hurtling me up into the sky.

I let my eyes roam around the control cabin. Most of its contents were quite familiar from photographs and films, and I knew what all the instruments were supposed to do. The control panel of a spaceship is not really very complicated because so much is done automatically.

The pilot was talking to the Port Control Tower over the radio, as they went through the pre-take-off routine together. Every so often a time-check broke through the conversations: "Minus fifteen minutes . . . Minus ten minutes . . . Minus five minutes." Though I'd heard this sort of thing so often before, it never fails to give me a thrill. And this time I wasn't watching it on TV—I was in the middle of it myself.

At last the pilot said "Over to Automatic" and threw a large red switch. He gave a sigh of relief, stretched his arms, and leaned back in his seat.

"That's always a nice feeling," he said. "No more work for the next hour!"

He didn't *really* mean that, of course. Although the robot controls would handle the ship from now on, he still had to see that everything was going according to plan. In an emergency, or if the robot pilot made an error, he would have to take over again.

The ship began to vibrate as the fuel pumps started to spin. A complicated pattern of intersecting lines had appeared on the TV screen, having something to do, I supposed, with the course the rocket was to follow. A row of tiny lights changed, one after another, from red to green. As the last light turned color, the pilot called to me swiftly, "Make sure you're lying quite flat."

I snuggled down into the couch and then, without any warning, felt as if someone had jumped on top of me. There was a tremendous roaring in my ears, and I seemed to weigh a ton. It required a definite effort to breathe; this was no longer something you could leave to your lungs and forget all about.

The feeling of discomfort lasted only a few seconds, then I grew accustomed to it. The ship's own motors had not yet started, and we were climbing under the thrust of the booster rockets, which would burn out and drop away after thirty seconds, when we were already many miles above the earth.

I could tell when this time came by the sudden slackening of weight. It lasted only a moment, then there was a subtly changed roaring as our own rockets started to fire. They would keep up their thunder for another five minutes. At the end of that time, we would be moving so swiftly that the earth could never drag us back.

The thrust of the rockets was now giving me more than three times my normal weight. As long as I stayed still, there was no real discomfort. As an experiment, I tried to see if I could raise my arm. It was very tiring, but not too difficult. Still, I was glad to let it drop back again. If necessary, I think I could have sat upright, but standing would have been quite impossible.

On the TV screen, the pattern of bright lines seemed unaltered. Now, however, there was a tiny spot creeping slowly upward—representing, I supposed, the ascending ship. I watched it intently, wondering if the motors would cut out when the spot reached the top of the screen.

Long before that happened, there came a series of short explosions, and the ship shuddered slightly. For one anxious moment, I thought that something had gone wrong. Then I realized what had happened: our drop tanks had been emptied, and the bolts holding them on had been severed. They were falling back behind us, and presently would plunge into the Pacific, somewhere in the great empty wastes between Tahiti and South America.

At last the thunder of the rockets began to lose its power, and the feeling of enormous weight ebbed away. The ship was easing itself into its final orbit, five hundred miles above the Equator. The motors had done their work and were now merely making the last adjustments to our course.

Silence returned as the rockets cut out completely. I could still feel the faint vibration of the fuel pumps as they idled to rest, but there was no sound whatsoever in the little cabin. My ears had been partially numbed by the roar of the rockets, and it took some minutes before I could hear properly again.

The pilot finished checking his instruments and then released himself from his seat. I watched him, fascinated, as he floated across to me.

"It will take you some time to get used to this," he said, as he unbuckled my safety strap. "The thing to remember is—always move gently. And never let go of one handhold until you've decided on the next."

Gingerly, I stood up. I grabbed the couch just in time to stop myself from zooming to the ceiling. Only, of course, it wasn't really the ceiling any more. "Up" and "down" had vanished completely. Weight had ceased to exist, and I had only to give myself a gentle push and move any way I wished.

It's a strange thing, but even now there are people who don't understand this business of "weightlessness." They seem to think it's something to do with being "outside the pull of gravity." That's nonsense, of course. In a space station or a coasting rocket five hundred miles up, gravity is nearly as powerful as it is down on the earth. The reason why you feel weightless is not because you're outside gravity, but because you're no longer resisting its pull. You could feel weightless, even down on earth, inside a freely falling elevator—as long as the fall lasted. An orbiting space station or rocket is in a kind of permanent fall—a "fall" that can last forever because it isn't toward the earth but *around* it.

"Careful, now!" warned the pilot. "I don't want you cracking your head against my instrument panel! If you want to have a look out of the window, hang on to this strap." I obeyed him, and peered through the little porthole, whose thick plastic was all that lay between me and nothingness.

Yes, I know that there have been so many films and photographs that everyone knows just what earth looks like from space. So I won't waste much time describing it. And to tell the truth, there wasn't a great deal to see, as my field of view was almost entirely filled by the Pacific Ocean.

Beneath me it was a surprisingly deep azure, which softened into a misty blue at the limits of vision. I asked the pilot how far away the horizon was.

"About two thousand miles," he replied. "You can see most of the way down to New Zealand and up to Hawaii. Quite a view, isn't it?"

Now that I had grown accustomed to the scale, I was able to pick out some of the Pacific islands, many showing their coral reefs quite clearly. A long way toward what I imagined was the west, the color of the ocean changed quite abruptly from blue to a vivid green. I realized I was looking at the enormous floating sea-farms that fed the continent of Asia, and which now covered a substantial part of all the oceans in the tropics.

The coast of South America was coming into sight when the pilot began to prepare for the landing on the Inner Station. (I know the word "landing" sounds peculiar, but it's the expression that's used. Out in space, many ordinary words have quite different meanings.) I was still staring out of the little porthole when I got the order to go back to my seat, so that I wouldn't fall around the cabin during the final maneuvers.

The TV screen was now a black rectangle, with a tiny double star shining near its center. We were about a hundred miles away from the station, slowly overhauling it. The two stars grew brighter and farther apart: additional faint satellites appeared sprinkled around them. I knew I was seeing the ships that were "in dock" at the moment, being refueled or overhauled.

Suddenly one of those faint stars burst into blazing light. A hundred miles ahead of us, one of the ships in that little fleet had started its motors and was pulling away from earth. I questioned the pilot.

"That would be the *Alpha Centauri*, bound for Venus," he replied. "She's a wonderful old wreck, but it's really time they pensioned her off. Now let me get on with my navigating. This is one job the robots can't do."

The Inner Station was only a few miles away when we started to put on the brakes. There was a high-pitched whistling from the steering jets in the nose, and for a moment a feeble sensation of weight returned. It lasted only a few seconds; then we had matched speeds and joined the station's other floating satellites.

Being careful to ask the pilot's permission, I got out of my couch and went to the window again. The earth was now on the other side of the ship, and I was looking out at the stars and the Space Station. It was such a staggering sight that I had to stare for a minute before it made any sense at all. I understood, now, the purpose of that orientation test the doctors had given me.

My first impression of the Inner Station was one of complete chaos. Floating there in space about a mile away from our ship was a great open latticework of spidery girders, in the shape of a flat disk. Here and there on its surface were spherical buildings of varying sizes, connected to each other by tubes wide enough for men to travel through. In the center of the disk was the largest sphere of all, dotted with the tiny eyes of portholes and with dozens of radio antennae jutting from it in all directions.

Several spaceships, some almost completely dismantled, were attached to the great disk at various points. They looked, I thought, very much like flies caught in a spiderweb. Men in space suits were working on them, and sometimes the glare of a welding torch would dazzle my eyes.

Other ships were floating freely, arranged in no particular system that I could discover, in the space around the station. Some of them were streamlined, winged vessels like the one that had brought me up from earth. Others were the true ships of space—assembled here outside the atmosphere and designed to ferry loads from world to world without ever landing on any planet. They were weird, flimsy constructions, usually with a pressurized spherical chamber for the crew and passengers, and larger tanks for the fuel. There was no streamlining of course: the cabins, fuel tanks and motors were simply linked together by thin struts. As I looked at these ships I

couldn't help thinking of some very old magazines I'd
once seen which showed our grandfather's idea of spaceships. They were all sleek, finned projectiles looking rather
like bombs. The artists who drew those pictures would
have been shocked by the reality: in fact they would probably not have recognized these queer objects as spaceships
at all.

I was wondering how we were going to get aboard the
station when something came sweeping into my field of
vision. It was a tiny cylinder, just big enough to hold a
man—and it *did* hold a man, for I could see his head
through the plastic panels covering one end of the device. Long, jointed arms projected from the machine's
body, and it was trailing a thin cable behind it. I could
just make out the faint, misty jet to the tiny rocket motor
which propelled this miniature spaceship.

The operator must have seen me staring out at him, for
he grinned back as he flashed by. A minute later there
came an alarming "clang" from the hull of our ship. The
pilot laughed at my obvious fright.

"That's only the towing cable being coupled. It's magnetic, you know. We'll start to move in a minute."

There was the feeblest of tugs, and our ship slowly ro-
tated until it was parallel to the great disk of the station.
The cable had been attached amidships, and the station
was hauling us in like an angler landing a fish. The pilot
pressed the button on the control panel, and there was
the whining of motors as our undercarriage lowered itself. *That* was not something you'd expect to see used in
space, but the idea was sensible enough. The shock absorbers were just the thing to take up the gentle impact
on making contact with the station.

We were wound in so slowly that it took almost ten
minutes to make the short journey. Then there was a slight
jar as we "touched down," and the journey was over.

"Well," grinned the pilot, "I hope you enjoyed the
trip. Or would you have liked some excitement?"

I looked at him cautiously, wondering if he was pulling my leg.

"It was quite exciting enough, thank you. What other sort of excitement could you supply?"

"Well, what about a few meteors, an attack by pirates, an invasion from outer space, or all the other things you read about in the fiction magazines?"

"*I* only read the serious books, like Richardson's *Introduction to Astronautics,* or Maxwell's *Modern Spaceships* —not magazine stories."

"I don't believe you," he replied promptly. "*I* read 'em, anyway, and I'm sure you do. You can't fool me."

He was right, of course. It was one of the first lessons I learned on the station. All the people out there have been hand-picked for intelligence as well as technical knowledge. If you weren't on the level, they'd spot it right away.

I was wondering how we were going to get out of the ship when there was a series of bangings and scrapings from the air lock, followed a moment later by an alarming hiss of air. It slowly died away, and presently, with a soft sucking noise, the inner door of the lock swung open.

"Remember what I told you about moving slowly," said the pilot, gathering up his log book. "The best thing is for you to hitch on to my belt and I'll tow you. Ready?"

I couldn't help thinking it wasn't a very dignified entry into the station. But it was safest to take no risks, so that was the way I traveled through the flexible, pressurized coupling that had been clamped on to the side of our ship. The pilot launched himself with a powerful kick, and I trailed along behind him. It was rather like learning to swim underwater, so much like it, in fact, that at first I had the panicky feeling that I'd drown if I tried to breathe.

Presently we emerged into a wide metal tunnel, one of the station's main passageways, I guessed. Cables and pipes ran along the walls, and at intervals we passed through great double doors with red EMERGENCY notices painted on them. I didn't think this was at all reassuring. We met only two people on our journey. They flashed by us with an effortless ease that filled me with envy, and made me determined to be just as skillful before I left the station.

"I'm taking you to Commander Doyle," the pilot explained to me. "He's in charge of training here and will be keeping an eye on you."

"What sort of man is he?" I asked anxiously.

"Don't you worry—you'll find out soon enough. Here we are."

We drifted to a halt in front of a circular door carrying the notice: "Cdr. R. Doyle, i/c Training. Knock and Enter." The pilot knocked and entered, still towing me behind him like a sack of potatoes.

I heard him say: "Captain Jones reporting, Mr. Doyle —with passenger." Then he shoved me in front of him and I saw the man he had been addressing.

He was sitting at a perfectly ordinary office desk, which was rather surprising in this place where nothing else seemed normal. And he looked like a prize fighter. I think he was the most powerfully built man I'd ever seen. Two huge arms covered most of the desk in front of him, and I wondered where he found clothes to fit, for his shoulders must have been over four feet across.

At first I didn't see his face clearly, for he was bending over some papers. Then he looked up, and I found myself staring at a huge red beard and two enormous eyebrows. It was some time before I really took in the rest of the face. It is so unusual to see a real beard nowadays that I couldn't help staring at it. Then I realized that Commander Doyle must have had some kind of accident, for there was a faint scar running diagonally right across his forehead. Considering how skilled our plastic surgeons are nowadays, the fact that it was still visible meant that the original injury must have been very serious.

Altogether, as you'll probably have gathered, Commander Doyle wasn't a very handsome man. But he was certainly a striking one, and my biggest surprise was still to come.

"So you're young Malcom, eh?" he said, in a pleasant,

quiet voice that wasn't half as fearsome as his appearance. "We've heard a great deal about you. O.K., Captain Jones—I'll take charge of him now."

The pilot saluted and glided away. For the next ten minutes Commander Doyle questioned me closely, building up a picture of my life and interests. I told him I'd been born in New Zealand and had lived for a few years in China, South Africa, Brazil and Switzerland, as my father—who is a journalist—moved from one job to another. We'd gone to Missouri because Mom was fed up with mountains and wanted a change. As families go these days, we hadn't traveled a great deal, and I'd never visited half the places all our neighbors seemed to know. Perhaps that was one reason why I wanted to go out into space.

When he had finished writing all this down, and adding many notes that I'd have given a good deal to read, Commander Doyle laid aside the old-fashioned fountain pen he was using and stared at me for a minute as if I was some peculiar animal. He drummed thoughtfully on the desk with his huge fingers, which looked as if they could tear their way through the material without much trouble. I was feeling a bit scared, and to make matters worse I'd drifted away from the floor and was floating helplessly in mid-air again. There was no way I could move anywhere unless I made myself ridiculous by trying to swim, which might or might not work. Then the commander gave a chuckle, and his face crinkled up into a vast grin.

"I think this may be quite amusing," he said. While I was still wondering if I dared to ask why, he continued, after glancing at some charts on the wall behind him: "Afternoon classes have just stopped. I'll take you to meet the boys." Then he grabbed a long metal tube that must have been slung underneath the desk, and launched himself out of his chair with a single jerk of his huge arm.

He moved so quickly that it took me completely by surprise. A moment later I just managed to stifle a gasp of amazement. For as he moved clear of the desk, I saw that Commander Doyle had no legs.

When you go to a new school or move into a strange district, there's always a confusing period so full of new experiences that you can never recall it clearly. My first day on the Space Station was like that. So much had never happened to me before in such a short time. It was not merely that I was meeting a lot of new people. I had to learn how to live all over again.

At first I felt as helpless as a baby. I couldn't judge the effort needed to make any movement. Although weight had vanished, *momentum* remained. It required force to start something moving and more force to stop it again. That was where the broomsticks came in.

Commander Doyle had invented them, and the name, of course, came from the old idea that once upon a time witches used to ride on broomsticks. We certainly rode around the station on ours. They consisted of one hollow tube sliding inside another. The two were connected by a powerful spring, one tube ending in a hook, the other in a wide rubber pad. That was all there was to it. If you wanted to move, you put the pad against the nearest wall and shoved. The recoil launched you into space, and when you arrived at your destination you let the spring absorb your velocity and so bring you to rest. Trying to stop yourself with your bare hands was liable to result in sprained wrists.

It wasn't quite as easy as it sounds, though, for if you weren't careful you could bounce right back the way you'd come.

It was a long time before I discovered what had happened to the commander. The scar he'd picked up in an ordinary motor crash when he was a young man, but the more serious accident was a different story, having occurred when he was on the first expedition to Mercury. He'd been quite an athlete, it seemed, so the loss of his legs must have been an even bigger blow to him than to most men. It was obvious why he had come to the station; it was the only place where he wouldn't be a cripple. Indeed, thanks to his powerfully developed arms, he was probably the most agile man in the station. He had lived here for the last ten years and would never return to earth, where he would be helpless again. He wouldn't even go over to any of the other space stations where they had gravity, and no one was ever tactless or foolish enough to suggest such a trip to him.

There were about a hundred people on board the Inner Station, ten of them apprentices a few years older than myself. At first they were a bit fed up at having me around, but after I'd had my fight with Ronnie Jordan everything was O.K., and they accepted me as one of the family. I'll tell you about that later.

The senior apprentice was a tall, quiet Canadian named Tim Benton. He never said much, but when he did speak everyone took notice. It was Tim who really taught me my way around the Inner Station, after Commander Doyle had handed me over to him with a few words of explanation.

"I suppose you know what we *do* up here?" he said doubtfully when the commander had left us.

"You refuel spaceships on their way out from earth, and carry out repairs and overhauls."

"Yes, that's our main job. The other stations—those farther out—have many other duties, but we needn't bother about that now. There's one important point I'd better make clear right away. This Inner Station of ours is really in two parts, with a couple of miles between them. Come and have a look."

He pulled me over to a port and I stared out into space. Hanging there against the stars, so close that it seemed I could reach out and touch it, was what seemed to be a giant flywheel. It was slowly turning on its axis, and as it revolved I could see the glitter of sunlight on its observation ports. I could not help comparing its smooth compactness with the flimsy, open girder work of the station in which I was standing—or, rather, floating. The great wheel had an axle, for jutting from its center was a long, narrow cylinder which ended in a curious structure I couldn't understand. A spaceship was slowly maneuvering near it.

"That's the Residential Station," said Benton disapprovingly. "It's nothing but a hotel. You've noticed that it's spinning. Because of that, it's got normal earth gravity at the rim, owing to centrifugal force. We seldom go over there; once you've got used to weightlessness, gravity's a nuisance. But all incoming passengers from Mars and the moon are transshipped there. It wouldn't be safe for them to go straight to earth after living in a much lower gravity field. In the Residential Station they can get acclimatized, as it were. They go in at the center, where there's no gravity, and work slowly out to the rim, where it's earth normal."

"How do they get aboard if the thing's spinning?" I asked.

"See that ship moving into position? If you look carefully, you'll see that the axle of the station isn't spinning; it's being driven by a motor against the station's spin so that it actually stands still in space. The ship can couple up to it and transfer passengers. The coupling's free to rotate, and once the axle revs up to match speed with the station, the passengers can go aboard. Sounds complicated, but it works well. And see if you can think of a better way!"

"Will I have a chance to go over there?" I asked.

"I expect it could be arranged—though I don't see much point in it. You might just as well be down on earth. That's the idea of the place, in fact."

I didn't press the point, and it wasn't until the very end of my visit that I was able to get over to the Residential Station, floating there only a couple of miles away.

It must have been quite a bother showing me around the station, because I had to be pushed or pulled most of the way until I'd found my "space legs." Once or twice Tim just managed to rescue me in time when I'd launched myself too vigorously and was about to plunge headlong into an obstacle. But he was very patient, and finally I

got the knack of things and was able to move around
fairly confidently.

It was several days before I really knew my way around
the great maze of interconnecting corridors and pressure chambers that was the Inner Station. In that first
trip I merely had a quick survey of its workshops, radio
equipment, power plant, air-conditioning gear, dormitories,
storage tanks and observatory. Sometimes it was hard to
believe that all this had been carried up into space and
assembled here five hundred miles above the earth. I
didn't know, until Tim mentioned it casually, that most
of the material in the station had actually come from the
moon. The moon's low gravity made it much more economical to ship equipment from there instead of from the
earth, despite the fact that earth was so much closer.

My first tour of inspection ended inside one of the air
locks. We stood in front of the great circular door, rest-
ing snugly on its rubber gaskets, which led into the outer
emptiness. Clamped to the walls around us were the space
suits, and I looked at them longingly. It had always
been one of my ambitions to wear one and to become a
tiny, self-contained world of my own.

"Do you think I'll have a chance of trying one on while
I'm here?" I asked.

Tim looked thoughtful; then he glanced at his watch.

"I'm not on duty for half an hour, and I want to collect
something I've left out at the rim. We'll go outside."

"But . . ." I gulped, my enthusiasm suddenly waning.
"Will it be safe? Doesn't it take a lot of training to use
one of these?"

He looked at me calmly. "Not *frightened,* are you?"

"Of course not."

"Well, let's get started."

Tim answered my question while he was showing me
how to get into the suit.

"It's quite true that it takes a lot of training before you
can operate one of these. I'm not going to let you try. You
sit tight inside and tag along with me. You'll be as safe
there as you are now, as long as you don't meddle with

the controls. Just to make sure, I'll lock them first."

I rather resented this, but didn't say anything. After all, he was the boss.

To most people, the word "space suit" conjures up a picture of something like a diving dress, in which a man can walk and use his arms. Such suits are, of course, used on places like the moon. But on a space station, where there's no gravity, your legs aren't much use anyway, because outside you have to blow yourself round with tiny rocket units.

For this reason, the lower part of the suit was simply a rigid cylinder. When I climbed inside it, I found that I could use my feet only to work some control pedals, which I was careful not to touch. There was a little seat, and a transparent dome covering the top of the cylinder gave me good visibility. I *could* use my hands and arms. Just below my chin there was a neat little control panel with a tiny keyboard and a few meters. If I wanted to handle anything outside, there were flexible sleeves through which I could push my arms. They ended in gloves which, although they seemed clumsy, enabled one to carry out quite delicate operations.

Tim threw some of the switches on my suit and clamped the transparent dome over my head. I felt rather like being inside a coffin with a view. Then he chose a suit for himself and attached it to mine by a thin nylon cord.

The inner door of the air lock thudded shut behind us, and I could hear the vibration of the pumps as the air was sucked back into the station. The sleeves of my suit began to stiffen slightly. Tim called across at me, his voice distorted after passing through our helmets.

"I won't switch on the radio yet. You should still be able to hear me. Listen to this." Then he went over to the familiar radio engineer's routine: "Testing, One, Two, Three, Four, Five . . ."

Around "Five" his voice began to fade. When he'd reached "Nine" I couldn't hear a thing, though his lips were still moving. There was no longer enough air around us to carry sound. The silence was quite uncanny, and I was relieved when talk came through the loud-speaker in my suit.

"I'm opening the outer door now. Don't make any movements—I'll do all that's necessary."

In that eerie silence, the great door slowly opened inward. I was floating freely now, and I felt a faint "tug" as the last traces of air puffed out into space. A circle of stars was ahead of me, and I could just glimpse the misty rim of earth to one side.

"Ready?" asked Tim.

"O.K.," I said, hoping that the microphone wouldn't betray my nervousness.

The towing line gave a tug as Tim switched on his jets, and we drifted out of the air lock. It was a terrifying sensation, yet one I would not have missed for anything. Although, of course, the words "up" and "down" had no meaning here, it seemed to me as if I were floating out through a hole in a great metal wall, with the earth at an immense distance below. My reason told me that I was perfectly safe, but all my instincts shouted, "You've a five-hundred-mile fall straight down beneath you!"

Indeed, when the earth filled half the sky, it was hard not to think of it as "down." We were in sunlight at the moment, passing across Africa, and I could see Lake Victoria and the great forests of the Congo. What would Livingstone and Stanley have thought, I wondered, if they had known that one day men would flash across the Dark Continent at 18,000 miles an hour? And the day of those great explorers was only two hundred years behind us. It had been a crowded couple of centuries. . . .

Though it was fascinating to look at earth, I found it was making me giddy, and so I swiveled round in my suit to concentrate on the station. Tim had now towed us well clear of it, and we were almost out among the halo of floating ships. I tried to forget about the earth, and now that I could no longer see it, it seemed natural enough to think of "down" as toward the station.

This is a knack everyone has to learn in space. You're liable to get awfully confused unless you pretend that *somewhere* is down. The important thing is to choose the most convenient direction, according to whatever you happen to be doing at the moment.

Tim had given us enough speed to make our little trip in a reasonable time, so he cut the jets and pointed out the sights as we drifted along. This bird's-eye view of the station completed the picture I'd already got from my tour inside, and I began to feel that I was really learning my way about.

The outer rim of the station was simply a flat webwork of girders trailing off into space. Here and there were large cylinders, pressurized workshops big enough to hold two or three men, and intended for any jobs that couldn't be handled in vacuum.

A spaceship with most of its plating stripped off was floating near the edge of the station, secured from drifting away by a couple of cords that would hardly have supported a man on earth. Several mechanics wearing suits like our own were working on the hull. I wished I could overhear their conversation and find what they were doing, but we were on a different wave length.

"I'm going to leave you here a minute," said Tim, unfastening the towing cord and clipping it to the nearest girder. "Don't do anything until I get back."

I felt rather foolish, floating around like a captive balloon, and was glad that no one took any notice of me. While waiting, I experimented with the fingers of my suit, and tried, unsuccessfully, to tie a simple knot in my towing cable. I found later that one *could* do this sort of thing, but it took practice. Certainly the men on the spaceship seemed to be handling their tools without any awkwardness, despite their gloves.

Suddenly it began to grow dark. Until this moment, the station and the ships floating beside it had been bathed in brilliant light from a sun so fierce that I had not dared to look anywhere near it. But now the sun was passing behind the earth as we hurtled across the night side of the planet. I turned my head, and there was a sight so splendid that it completely took away my breath. Earth was now a huge, black disk eclipsing the stars, but all along one edge was a glorious crescent of golden light, shrinking even as I watched. I was looking back upon the line of the sunset, stretching for a thousand miles across Africa. At its center was a great halo of dazzling gold, where a thin sliver of sun was still visible. It dwindled and vanished; the crimson afterglow of the sunset contracted swiftly along the horizon until it too disappeared. The whole thing lasted not more than two minutes, and the men working around me took not the slightest notice of it. After all, in time one gets used even to the most wonderful sights, and the station circled the earth so swiftly that sunset occurred every hundred minutes.

It was not completely dark, for the moon was half full, looking no brighter or closer than it did from earth. And the sky was so crowded with millions of stars, all shining without a trace of twinkling, that I wondered how anyone could ever have spoken of the "blackness" of space.

I was so busy looking for the other planets (and failing to find them) that I never noticed Tim's return until my towrope began to tug. Slowly we moved back toward the center of the station, and in such utter silence that it hardly seemed real. I closed my eyes for a minute, but the scene hadn't changed when I opened them. There was the great black shield of earth—no, not quite black, for I could see the oceans glimmering in the moonlight. The same light made the slim girders around me gleam like the threads of a ghostly spider's web, a web sprinkled with myriads of stars.

This was the moment when I really knew that I had reached space at last, and that nothing else could ever be the same again.

3   THE MORNING STAR

◆◆

"Now on station Four, do you know what our biggest trouble used to be?" asked Norman Powell.

"No," I replied, which was what I was supposed to say.

"Mice," he exclaimed solemnly. "Believe it or not! Some of them got loose from the biology labs, and before you knew where you were, they were all over the place."

"I don't believe a word of it," interrupted Ronnie Jordan.

"They were so small they could get into all the air shafts," continued Norman, unabashed. "You could hear them scuttling around happily whenever you put your ear to the walls. There was no need for them to make holes—every room had half a dozen already provided, and you can guess what they did to the ventilation. But we got them in the end, and do you know how we did it?"

"You borrowed a couple of cats."

Norman gave Ronnie a superior look.

"That *was* tried, but cats don't like zero gravity. They were no good at all; the mice used to laugh at them. No; we used *owls*. You should have seen them fly! Their wings worked just as well as ever, of course, and they used to do the most fantastic things. It took them only a few months to get rid of the mice."

He sighed.

"The problem then, of course, was to get rid of the owls. We did this . . ."

I never learned what happened next, for the rest of the gang decided they'd had enough of Norman's tall stories and everybody launched at him simultaneously. He disappeared in the middle of a slowly revolving sphere of bodies that drifted noisily around the cabin. Only Tim Benton, who never got mixed up in these vulgar brawls, remained quietly studying, which was what everybody else was supposed to be doing.

Every day all the apprentices met in the classroom to hear a lecture by Commander Doyle or one of the station's technical officers. The commander had suggested that I attend these talks, and a suggestion from him was not very different from an order. He thought that I might pick up some useful knowledge, which was true enough. I could understand about a quarter of what was said, and spent the rest of the time reading something from the station's library of ultra-lightweight books.

After the classes there was a thirty-minute study period, and from time to time some studying *was* actually done. These intervals were much more useful to me than the lessons themselves, for the boys were always talking about their jobs and the things they had seen in space. Some of them had been out here for two years, with only a few short trips down to earth.

Of course, a lot of the tales they told me were, shall I say, slightly exaggerated. Norman Powell, our prize humorist, was always trying to pull my leg. At first I fell for some of his yarns, but later I learned to be more cautious.

There were also, I'd discovered, some interesting tricks and practical jokes that could be played in space. One of the best involved nothing more complicated than an ordinary match. We were in the classroom one afternoon when Norman suddenly turned to me and said, "Do you know how to test the air to see if it's breathable?"

"If it wasn't, I suppose you'd soon know," I replied.

"Not at all—you might be knocked out too quickly to do anything about it. But there's a simple test which has been used on earth for ages, in mines and caves. You just carry a flame ahead of you, and if it goes out—well, you go out too, as quickly as you can!"

He fumbled in his pocket and extracted a box of matches. I was mildly surprised to see something so old-fashioned aboard the station.

"In here, of course," Norman continued, "a flame will burn properly. But if the air was bad it would go out at once."

He absent-mindedly struck a match on the box, and it burst into light. A flame formed around the head, and I leaned forward to look at it closely. It was a very odd flame, not long and pointed but quite spherical. Even as I watched, it dwindled and died.

It's funny how the mind works, for up to that moment I'd been breathing comfortably, yet now I seemed to be suffocating. I looked at Norman, and said nervously, "Try it again—there must be something wrong with the match."

Obediently he struck another, which expired as quickly as the first.

"Let's get out of here," I gasped. "The air purifier must have packed up." Then I saw that the others were grinning at me.

"Don't panic, Roy," said Tim. "There's a simple answer." He grabbed the matchbox from Norman.

"The air's perfectly O.K. But if you think about it, you'll see that it's impossible for a flame to burn out here.

Since there's no gravity and everything stays put, the smoke doesn't rise and the flame just chokes itself. The only way it will keep burning is if you do this."

He struck another match, but instead of holding it still, kept it moving slowly through the air. It left a trail of smoke behind it, and kept on burning until only the stump was left.

"It was entering fresh air all the time," Tim continued. "So it didn't choke itself with burnt gases. And if you think this is just an amusing trick of no practical importance, you're wrong. It means we've got to keep the air in the station on the move, otherwise *we'd* soon go the same way as that flame. Norman, will you switch on the ventilators again, now that you've had your little joke?"

Joke or not, it was a very effective lesson. But it made me all the more determined that one of these days I was going to get my own back on Norman. Not that I disliked him, but I *was* getting a little tired of his sense of humor.

Someone gave a shout from the other side of the room.

"The *Canopus* is leaving!"

We all rushed to the small circular windows and looked out into space. It was some time before I could manage to see anything, but presently I wormed my way to the front and pressed my face against the thick transparent plastic.

The *Canopus* was the largest liner on the Mars run, and she had been here for some weeks having her routine overhaul. During the last two days fuel and passengers had been going aboard, and she had now drifted away from the station until we were separated by a space of several miles. Like the Residential Station, the *Canopus* slowly revolved to give the passengers a sense of gravity. She was shaped rather like a giant doughnut, the cabins and living quarters forming a ring around the power plant and drive units. During the voyage the ship's spin would be gradually reduced, so that by the time her passengers reached Mars they would already be accustomed to the right gravity. On the homeward journey, just the reverse would happen.

The departure of a spaceship from an orbit is not nearly so spectacular as a take-off from earth. It all happens in utter silence, of course, and it also happens very slowly. Nor is there any flame and smoke. All that I could see was a faint pencil of mist jetting from the drive units. The great radiator fins began to glow cherry red, then white hot, as the waste heat from the power plant flooded away into space. The liner's thousands of tons were gradually picking up speed, though it would be many hours before she gained enough velocity to escape from earth. The rocket that had carried me up to the station had traveled at a hundred times the acceleration of the *Canopus,* but the great liner could keep her drive units thrusting gently for weeks on end, to build up a final speed of almost half a million miles an hour.

After five minutes, she was several miles away and moving at an appreciable velocity, pulling out away from our own orbit into the path leading to Mars. I stared hungrily after her, wondering when I too would travel on such a journey. Norman must have seen my expression, for he chuckled and said:

"Thinking of stowing away on the next ship? Well, forget it. It can't be done. Oh, I know it's a favorite dodge in fiction, but it has never happened in practice. There are too many safeguards. And do you know what they'd do to a stowaway if they did find one?"

"No," I said, trying not to show too much interest—for to tell the truth I had been thinking along these lines.

Norman rubbed his hand ghoulishly. "Well, an extra person on board would mean that much less food and oxygen for everyone else, and it would upset the fuel calculations too. So he'd simply be pushed overboard."

"Then it's just as well that no one ever has stowed away."

"It certainly is—but of course a stowaway wouldn't have a chance. He'd be spotted before the voyage began. There just isn't room to hide in a spaceship."

I filed this information away for future reference. It might come in handy someday.

Space Station One was a big place, but the apprentices didn't spend all their time aboard it, as I quickly found out. They had a club room which must have been unique, and it was some time before I was allowed to visit it.

Not far from the station was a veritable museum of astronautics, a floating graveyard of ships that had seen their day and been withdrawn from service. Most of them had been stripped of their instruments and were no more than skeletons. On earth, of course, they would have rusted away long ago, but here in vacuum they would remain bright and untarnished forever.

Among these derelicts were some of the great pioneers —the first ship to land on Venus, the first to reach the satellites of Jupiter, the first to circle Saturn. At the end of their long voyages, they had entered the five-hundred-mile orbit round earth and the ferry rockets had come up to take off their crews. They were still here where they had been abandoned, never to be used again.

All, that is, except the *Morning Star*. As everyone knows, she made the first circumnavigation of Venus, back in 1985. But very few people know that she was still in an excellent state of repair, for the apprentices had adopted her, made her their private headquarters, and, for their own amusement, had got her into working condition again. Indeed, they believed she was at least as good as new and were always trying to "borrow" enough rocket fuel to make a short trip. They were very hurt because no one would let them have any.

Commander Doyle, of course, knew all about this and quite approved of it. After all, it was good training. Sometimes he came over to the *Morning Star* to see how things were getting on, but it was generally understood that the ship was private property. You had to have an invitation before you were allowed aboard. Not until I'd been around for some days, and had become more or less accepted as one of the gang, did I have a chance of making the trip over to the *Morning Star*.

It was the longest journey I had made outside the station, for the graveyard was about five miles away, moving in the same orbit as the station but a little ahead of it. I don't quite know how to describe the curious vehicle in which we made the trip. It had been constructed out of junk salvaged from other ships, and was really nothing more than a pressurized cylinder, large enough to hold a dozen people. A low-powered rocket unit had been bolted to one end, there were a few auxiliary jets for steering, a simple air lock, a radio to keep in touch with the station— and that was all. This peculiar vessel could make the hop across to the *Morning Star* in about ten minutes, being capable of achieving a top speed of about thirty miles an hour. She had been christened *The Skylark of Space,* a name apparently taken from a famous old science fiction story.

The *Skylark* was usually kept parked at the outer rim of the station, where she wouldn't get in anybody's way. When she was needed, a couple of the apprentices would go out in space suits, loosen her mooring lines, and tow her to the nearest air lock. Then she would be coupled up and you could go aboard through the connecting tube, just as if you were entering a real space liner.

My first trip in the *Skylark* was a very different experience from the climb up from earth. She looked so ramshackle that I expected her to fall to pieces at any moment, though in fact she had a perfectly adequate margin of safety. With ten of us aboard, her little cabin was distinctly crowded, and when the rocket motor started up, the gentle acceleration made us all drift slowly toward the rear of the ship. The thrust was so feeble that it made me weigh only about a pound, quite a contrast to the take-off weight from earth, where I could have sworn I weighed a ton! After a minute or so of this leisurely progress, we shut off the drive and drifted freely for another ten minutes, by which time a further brief burst of power brought us neatly to rest at our destination.

There was plenty of room inside the *Morning Star;* after all she had been the home of five men for almost two years.

Their names were still there, scratched on the paint work in the control cabin, and the sight of those signatures took my imagination back almost a hundred years, to the great pioneering days of spaceflight, when even the moon was a new world and no one had yet reached any of the planets.

Despite the ship's age, everything inside the control room still seemed bright and new. The instrument board, as far as I could tell, might have belonged to a ship of my own time. Tim Benton stroked the panel gently. "As good as new!" he said, with obvious pride in his voice. "I'd guarantee to take you to Venus any day!"

I got to know the *Morning Star* controls pretty well. It was safe to play with them, of course, since the fuel tanks were empty and all that happened when one pressed the "Main Drive—Fire!" button was that a red light lit up. Still, it was exciting to sit in the pilot's seat and to daydream with my hands on the controls.

A little workshop had been fitted up just aft of the main fuel tanks, and a lot of modelmaking went on here, as well as a good deal of serious engineering. Several of the apprentices had designed gadgets they wanted to try out, and were seeing if they worked in practice before they took them any farther. Karl Hasse, our mathematical genius, was trying to build some new form of navigational device, but as he always hid it as soon as anybody came along, no one knew just what it was supposed to do.

I learned more about spaceships while I was crawling around inside the *Morning Star* than I ever did from books or lectures. It was true that she was nearly a century old, but although the details have altered, the main principles of spaceship design have changed less than one might expect. You still have to have pumps, fuel tanks, air purifiers, temperature regulators, and so on. The gadgets may change, but the jobs they must do remain the same.

The information I absorbed aboard the *Morning Star* was not merely technical by any means. I finished my training in weightlessness here, and I also learned to fight in free-fall. Which brings me to Ronnie Jordan.

Ronnie was the youngest of the apprentices, about two years older than myself. He was a boisterous, fair-haired Australian—at least, he'd been born in Sydney but had spent most of his life in Europe. As a result, he spoke three or four languages, sometimes accidentally slipping from one to the other.

He was good-natured and lighthearted, and gave the impression that he'd never quite got used to zero gravity but still regarded it as a great joke. At any rate, he was always trying out new tricks, such as making a pair of wings and seeing how well he could fly with them. (The answer was—not very well. But perhaps the wings weren't properly designed.) Because of his high spirits, he was always getting into good-humored fights with the other boys, and a fight under free-fall conditions is fascinating to watch.

The first problem, of course, is to catch your opponent, which isn't easy, because if he refused to cooperate, he can shoot off in so many directions. But even if he decides to play, there are further difficulties. Any kind of boxing is almost impossible, since the first blow would send you flying apart. So the only practicable form of combat is wrestling. It usually starts with the two fighters floating in mid-air, as far as possible from any solid object. They grasp wrists, with their arms fully extended; after that it's difficult to see exactly what happens. The air is full of flying limbs and slowly rotating bodies. By the rules of the game, you've won if you can keep your opponent pinned against any wall for a count of five. This is much more difficult than it sounds, for he only has to give a good heave to send both of you flying out into the room again. Remember that, since there's no gravity, you can't just sit on your victim until your weight tires him out.

My first fight with Ronnie arose out of a political argument. Perhaps it seems funny that out in space earth's politics matter at all. In a way they don't, at least, no one worries whether you're a citizen of the Atlantic Federation, the Panasiatic Union or the Pacific Confederacy. But there were plenty of arguments about which country was the best to live in, and as most of us had traveled a good deal, each had different ideas.

When I told Ronnie that he was talking nonsense, he said, "Them's fightin' words," and before I knew what had happened I was pinned in a corner while Norman Powell lazily counted up to ten to give me a chance. I couldn't escape, because Ronnie had his feet braced firmly against the other two walls forming the corner of the cabin.

The next time I did slightly better, but Ronnie still won easily. Not only was he stronger than I was, but I didn't have the technique.

In the end, however, I did succeed in winning—just once. It took a lot of careful planning, and maybe Ron had become overconfident as well.

I realized that if I let him get me in a corner I was done for. He could use his favorite "starfish" trick and pin me down, by bracing himself against the walls where they came together. On the other hand, if I stayed out in the open, his superior strength and skill would soon force me into an unfavorable position. It was necessary, therefore, to think of some way of neutralizing his advantages.

I thought about the problem a lot before discovering the answer, and then I put in a good deal of practice when nobody else was around, for it needed very careful timing.

At last I was ready. We were seated round the little table bolted to one end of the *Morning Star*'s cabin—the end which was usually regarded as the floor. Ron was opposite me, and we'd been arguing in a good-natured manner for some time. It was obvious that a fight was about to start at any minute. When Ron began to unbuckle his seat straps I knew it was time to take off.

He'd just unfastened himself when I shouted, "Come and get me!" and launched myself straight at the "ceiling," fifteen feet away. This was the bit that had to be timed carefully. Once he'd judged the course I was taking, Ron kicked himself off a fraction of a second after me.

In free orbit, once you'd launched yourself on a definite path, you can't stop until you bump into something again. Ron expected to meet me on the ceiling; what he *didn't* expect was that I'd get only halfway there. For my foot was tucked in a loop of cord that I'd thoughtfully fastened to the floor. I'd gone only a couple of yards when I jerked to a stop, dragging myself back the way I'd come. Ron couldn't do anything but sail right on. He was so surprised at seeing me jerk back that he rolled over while ascending, to watch what had happened, and hit the ceiling with quite a thud. He hadn't recovered from this when I launched myself again, and this time I *didn't* hang on to the cord. Ron was still off balance as I came up like a meteor. He couldn't get out of the way in time and so I knocked the wind out of him. It was easy to hold him down for the count of five; in fact, Norman got to ten before Ron showed any signs of life. I was beginning to get a bit worried when he finally started to stir.

Perhaps it wasn't a very famous victory, and a number of people thought I'd cheated. Still, there was nothing against this sort of thing in the rules.

It wasn't a trick I could use twice, and Ron got his own back next time. But after all, he *was* older than I.

Some of our games weren't quite so rough. We played a lot of chess, with magnetic men, but as I'm no good at this, it wasn't much fun for me. About the only game at which I could always win was "swimming"—not swimming in water, of course, but swimming in air.

This was so exhausting that we didn't do it very often. You need a fairly large room, and the competitors had to start floating in a line, well away from the nearest wall. The idea was to reach the winning post by clawing your way through the air. It was much like swimming through water, but a lot harder and slower. For some reason I was better at it than the others, which is rather odd, because I'm not much good at ordinary swimming.

Still, I mustn't give the impression that all our time was

spent in the *Morning Star*. There is plenty of work for everyone on a space station, and perhaps because of this the staff made the most of their time off. And—this is a curious point that isn't very well known—we had more opportunities for amusement than you might think because we needed very little sleep. That's one of the effects of zero gravity. All the time I was in space, I don't think I ever had more than four hours of continuous sleep.

I was careful never to miss one of Commander Doyle's lectures, even when there were other things I wanted to do. Tim had advised me, tactfully, that it would make a good impression if I was always there—and the commander was a good speaker, anyway. Certainly I'm never likely to forget the talk on meteors which he gave to us.

Looking back on it, that's rather funny, because I thought the lecture was going to be pretty dull. The opening was interesting enough, but it soon bogged down in statistics and tables. You know what meteors are—tiny particles of matter which whirl through space and burn up through friction when they hit the earth's atmosphere. The huge majority are much smaller than sand grains, but sometimes quite large ones, weighing many pounds, come tumbling down into the atmosphere. And on very rare occasions, hundred or even thousand-ton giants come crashing to earth and do considerable local damage.

In the early days of spaceflight many people were nervous about meteors. They didn't realize just how big space was and thought that leaving the protective blanket of the atmosphere would be like entering a machine-gun barrage. Today we know better; though meteors are not a serious danger, small ones occasionally puncture stations or ships, and it's necessary to do something about them.

My attention had strayed while Commander Doyle talked about meteor streams and covered the blackboard with calculations showing how little solid matter there really was in the space between the planets. I became more interested when he began to say what would happen if a meteor ever did hit us.

"You have to remember," he said, "that because of its speed a meteor doesn't behave like a slow-moving object such as a rifle bullet, which moves at a mere mile a second. If a small meteor hits a solid object—even a piece of paper—it turns into a cloud of incandescent vapor. That's one reason why this station has a double hull: the outer shell provides almost complete protection against any meteors we're ever likely to meet.

"But there's still a faint possibility that a big one might go through both walls and make a fairly large hole. Even that needn't be serious. The air would start rushing out, of course, but every room that has a wall toward space is fitted with one of these."

He held up a circular disk, looking very much like a saucepan cover with a rubber flange around it. I'd often seen these disks, painted a bright yellow, clipped to the walls of the station, but hadn't given them much thought.

"This is capable of taking care of leaks up to six inches in diameter. All you have to do is to place it against the wall near the hole and slide it along until it covers the leak. Never try to clamp the disk straight over the hole. Once it's in place, the air pressure will keep it there until a permanent repair can be made."

He tossed the disk down into the class.

"Have a look at it and pass it around. Any questions?"

I wanted to ask what would happen if the hole was more than six inches across, but was afraid this might be regarded as a facetious question. Glancing around the class to see if anyone else looked like breaking the silence, I noticed that Tim Benton wasn't there. It was unusual for him to be absent, and I wondered what had happened to him. Perhaps he was helping someone on an urgent job elsewhere in the station.

I had no further chance to puzzle over Tim's whereabouts. For at that precise moment there was a sudden, sharp explosion, quite deafening in that confined space. It was followed instantly by the terrifying, high-pitched, scream of escaping air, air rushing through a hole that had suddenly appeared in the wall of the classroom.

4 A PLAGUE OF PIRATES

❖❖❖❖❖❖❖❖❖❖❖❖❖❖❖❖❖❖❖❖❖❖❖❖❖❖❖❖❖❖❖❖❖❖

FOR A MOMENT, as the outrushing air tore at our clothes and tugged us toward the wall, we were far too surprised to do anything except stare at the ragged puncture scarring the white paint. Everything had happened too quickly for me to be frightened—that came later. Our paralysis lasted for a couple of seconds; then we all moved at once. The sealing plate had been lying on Norman Powell's desk, and everyone made toward it. There was a moment of confused pushing, then Norman shouted above the shriek of air, "Out of my way!" He launched himself across the room, and the air current caught him like a straw in a millrace, slamming him into the wall. I watched in helpless fascination as he fought to prevent himself being sucked against the hole. Then, as suddenly as it had begun, the whistling roar ceased. Norman had managed to slide the seal into place.

For the first time, I turned to see what Commander

Doyle had been doing during the crisis. To my astonishment, he was still sitting quietly at his desk. What was more, there was a smile on his face, and a stop-watch in his hand. A dreadful suspicion began to creep into my mind, a suspicion that became a certainty in the next few moments. The others were also staring at him, and there was a long, icy silence. Then Norman coughed, and very ostentatiously rubbed his elbow where he had bruised it against the wall. If he could have managed a limp under zero gravity, I'm sure he'd have done so as he went back to his desk. When he reached there, he relieved his feelings by grabbing the elastic band that held his writing pad in place, pulling it away and letting it go with a "Twack!" The commander continued to grin.

"Sorry if you've hurt yourself, Norman," he remarked. "I really must congratulate you on the speed with which you acted. It took you only five seconds to get to the wall, which was very good when one allows for the fact that everybody else was getting in the way."

"Thank you, sir," replied Norman, with quite unnecessary emphasis on the "sir." I could see he still didn't like the idea of having a practical joke played on him for a change. "But wasn't it rather a dangerous—er—trick to play?"

"Not at all. If you want the technical details, there's a three-inch pipe around that hole, with a stopcock at the end of it. Tim is sitting out there in a space suit, and if we hadn't sealed the leak inside ten seconds, he'd have closed the tap and cut off the flow."

"How was the hole made?" someone asked.

"Just a small explosive charge, a very small one," replied the commander. His grin had vanished and he had become quite serious again.

"I didn't do this just for fun. One day you may run into a real leak, and this test may make all the difference because you'll know what to do. As you've seen, a puncture this size can make quite a draft and could empty a room in half a minute. But it's easy enough to deal with if you act quickly and don't panic."

He turned to Karl Hasse, who, like the good student he was, always sat in the front row.

"Karl, I noticed you were the only one who never moved. Why?"

In his dry, precise voice, Karl answered without any hesitation.

"It was simple deduction. The chance of being hit by a large meteor is, as you had explained, inconceivably rare. The chance of being hit by one just when you'd finished talking about them was—well, so rare that it's nearly impossible. So I knew there was no danger, and that you must be conducting some sort of test. That was why I just sat and waited to see what would happen."

We all looked at Karl, feeling a little sheepish. I suppose he was right; he always was. It didn't help to make him any more popular.

One of the biggest excitements of life in a space station is the arrival of the mail rocket from earth. The great interplanetary liners can come and go, but they're not so important as the tiny, bright yellow ships that keep the crews of the station in touch with home. Radio messages are all very well, but they can't compare with letters and, above all, parcels from earth.

The station mail department was a cubby-hole near one of the air locks, and a small crowd usually gathered there even before the rocket had coupled up. As soon as the mailbags came aboard, they would be ripped open and some high-speed sorting would take place. Then the crowd would disperse, everyone hugging his correspondence or else saying, "Oh, well, I wasn't expecting anything this time . . ."

The lucky man who got a parcel couldn't keep it to himself for long. Space mail is expensive, and a parcel usually meant one of those little luxuries you couldn't normally obtain on the station.

I was very surprised to find that I had quite a pile of letters waiting for me after the first rocket arrived—most of them from perfect strangers. The great majority were from boys of my own age who'd heard about me, or maybe had seen my TV appearances, and wanted to know all about life on the station. If I'd answered every one, there'd have been no time for anything else. What was worse, I couldn't possibly *afford* to acknowledge them, even if I had the time. The postage would have taken all my spare cash.

I asked Tim what I'd better do about it. He looked at some of the letters and replied:

"Maybe I'm being cynical, but I think most of them are after space-mail stamps. If you feel you *ought* to acknowledge them, wait until you get back to earth. It'll be much cheaper."

That was what I did, though I'm afraid a lot of people were disappointed.

There was also a parcel from home, containing a good assortment of candy and a letter from Mom telling me to be sure to wrap up tight against the cold. I didn't say anything about the letter, but the rest of the parcel made me very popular for a couple of days.

There cannot be many people on earth who have never seen the TV serial "Dan Drummond, Space Detective." Most of them, at some time or another, must have watched Dan tracking down interplanetary smugglers and assorted crooks, or have followed his never-ending battle with Black Jarvis, most diabolical of space pirates.

When I came to the station, one of my minor surprises was discovering how popular Dan Drummond was among the staff. If they were off duty, and often when they weren't, they never missed an instalment of his adventures. Of course, they all pretended that they tuned in for the laughs, but that wasn't quite true. For one thing, "Dan Drummond" isn't half so ridiculous as many of the other TV serials. In fact, on the technical side it's pretty well done and the producers obviously get expert advice, even if they don't always use it. There's more than a suspicion that someone aboard the station helps with the script, but nobody has ever been able to prove this. Even Commander Doyle has come under suspicion, though it's most unlikely that anyone will ever accuse him outright.

We were all particularly interested in the current episode, as it concerned a space station supposed to be orbiting Venus. Blackie's marauding cruiser, *The Queen of Night*, was running short of fuel, so the pirates were planning to raid the station and replenish their tanks. If they could make off with some loot and hostages at the same time, so much the better. When the last instalment of the serial had ended, the pirate cruiser, painted jet black, was creeping up on the unsuspecting station, and we were all wondering what was going to happen next.

There has never been such a thing as piracy in space, and since no one except a multi-million combine can afford to build ships and supply them with fuel, it's difficult to see how Black Jarvis could hope to make a living. This didn't spoil our enjoyment of the serial, but it sometimes caused fierce arguments about the prospects for spatial crime. Peter van Holberg, who spent a lot of his time reading lurid magazines and watching the serials, was sure that *something* could be done if one was really determined. He amused himself by inventing all sorts of ingenious crimes and asking us what was to stop a person from getting away with them. We felt that he had missed his true vocation.

Black Jarvis' latest exploit made Peter unusually thoughtful, and for a day or so he went around working out just how valuable the contents of the station would be to an interplanetary desperado. It made an impressive figure, especially when one included the freight charges. If Peter's mind hadn't already been working along these lines, he would never have noticed the peculiar behavior of the *Cygnus*.

In addition to the spaceships on the regular, scheduled runs, ships on special missions touched at the station about two or three times a month. Usually they were engaged on scientific research projects, occasionally something really exciting like an expedition to the outer planets. Whatever it was they were doing, everyone aboard the station always knew all about it.

But no one knew much about the *Cygnus,* except that she was down in Lloyd's Register as a medium freighter and was about due to be withdrawn from service, since she had been in operation for almost five years without a major overhaul. It attracted little surprise when she came up to the station and anchored (yes, that's the expression still used) about ten miles away. This distance was greater than usual, but that might only mean that she had an ultracautious pilot. And there she stayed. All attempts to discover what she was doing failed completely. She had a crew of two. We knew that because they jetted over in their suits and reported to Control. They gave no clearance date and refused to state their business, which was unheard of but not illegal.

Naturally this started many theories circulating. One was that the ship had been chartered secretly by Prince Edward, who as everybody knew had been trying to get out into space for years. It seems the British Parliament won't let him go, the heir to the throne being considered too valuable to risk on such dangerous amusements as spaceflight. However, the Prince is such a determined young man that no one will be surprised if he turns up on Mars one day, having disguised himself and signed on with the crew. If he ever attempts such a journey, he'll find plenty of people ready to help him.

But Peter had a much more sinister theory. The arrival of a mysterious and untalkative spaceship fitted in perfectly with his ideas on interplanetary crime. If you wanted to rob a space station, he argued, how else would you set about it?

We laughed at him, pointing out that the *Cygnus* had done her best to arouse suspicion rather than allay it. Besides, she was a small ship and couldn't carry a very large crew. The two men who'd come across to the station were probably all she had aboard.

By this time, however, Peter was so wrapped up in his theories that he wouldn't listen to reason, and because it amused us we let him carry on and even encouraged him. But we didn't take him seriously.

The two men from the *Cygnus* would come aboard the station at least once a day to collect any mail from earth and to read the papers and magazines in the rest room. That was natural enough, if they had nothing else to do, but Peter thought it highly suspicious. It proved, according to him, that they were reconnoitering the station and getting to know their way around. "To lead the way, I suppose," said someone sarcastically, "for a boarding party with cutlasses."

Then, unexpectedly, Peter turned up fresh evidence that made us take him a little more seriously. He discovered from the Signals Section that our mysterious guests were continually receiving messages from earth, using their own radio on a wave band not allocated for official or commercial services. There was nothing illegal about that, since they were operating in one of the "free ether" bands, but once again it was unusual. *And they were using code*. That was most unusual.

Peter was very excited about all this. "It proves that there's something funny going on," he said belligerently. "No one engaged on honest business would behave like this. I won't say that they're going in for something as old-fashioned as piracy. But what about drug smuggling?"

"I should hardly think that the number of drug addicts in the Martian and Venusian colonies would make this very profitable," put in Tim Benton mildly.

"I wasn't thinking of smuggling in *that* direction," retorted Peter scornfully. "Suppose someone's discovered a drug on one of the planets and is smuggling it back to earth?"

"You got *that* idea from the last Dan Drummond adventure but two," said somebody. "You know, the one they had on last year—all about the Venus lowlands."

"There's only one way of finding out," continued Peter stubbornly. "I'm going over to have a look. Who'll come with me?"

There were no volunteers. I'd have offered to go, but I knew he wouldn't accept me.

"What, all afraid?" Peter taunted.

"Just not interested," replied Norman. "I've got better ways of wasting my time."

Then, to our surprise, Karl Hasse came forward.

"I'll go," he said. "I'm getting fed up with the whole affair, and it's the only way we can stop Peter from harping on it."

It was against safety regulations for Peter to make a trip of this distance by himself, so unless Karl had volunteered he would have had to drop the idea.

"When are you going?" asked Tim.

"They come over for their mail every afternoon, and when they're both aboard the station we'll wait for the next eclipse period and slip out."

That would be the fifty minutes when the station was passing through the earth's shadow. It was very difficult to see small objects at any distance then, so there was little chance of detection. They would also have some difficulty in finding the *Cygnus,* since she would reflect very little starlight and would probably be invisible from more than a half mile away. Tim Benton pointed this out.

"I'll borrow a 'beeper' from Stores," replied Peter. "Joe Evans will let me sign for one."

A beeper is a tiny radar set, not much bigger than a hand torch, which is used to locate objects that have drifted away from the station. It's got a range of a few miles on anything as large as a space suit and could pick up a ship a lot farther away. You wave it around in space, and when its beam hits anything you hear a series of "beeps." The closer you get to the reflecting object, the faster the beeps come, and with a little practice you can judge distances pretty accurately.

Tim Benton finally gave his grudging consent for this adventure, on condition that Peter keep in radio touch all the time and tell him exactly what was happening. So I heard the whole thing over the loud-speaker in one of the workshops. It was easy to imagine that I was out there with Peter and Karl in that star-studded darkness with the great shadowy earth below me, and the station slowly receding behind.

They had taken a careful sight of the *Cygnus* while she was still visible by reflected sunlight and had waited for five minutes after we'd gone into eclipse before launching themselves in the right direction. Their course was so accurate that they had no need to use the beeper: the *Cygnus* came looming up at them at just about the calculated moment, and they slowed to a halt.

"All clear," reported Peter, and I could sense the excitement in his voice. "There's no sign of life."

"Can you see through the ports?" asked Tim. There was silence for a while, apart from heavy breathing and an occasional metallic click from the space suit's controls. Then we heard a "bump" and an exclamation from Peter.

"That was pretty careless," came Karl's voice. "If there was anyone else inside, they'll think they've run into an asteroid."

"I couldn't help it," protested Peter. "My foot slipped on the jet control." Then we heard some scrabbling noises as he made his way over the hull.

"I can't see into the cabin," he reported. "It's too dark. But there's certainly no one around. I'll go aboard. Is everything O.K.?"

"Yes. Our two suspects are playing chess in the recreation room. Norman's looked at the board and says they'll be a long time yet." Tim chuckled. I could see he was enjoying himself and taking the whole affair as a great joke. I was beginning to find it quite exciting.

"Beware of booby traps," Tim continued. "I'm sure no experienced pirates would walk out of their ship and leave it unguarded. Maybe there's a robot waiting in the air lock with a ray gun!"

Even Peter thought this unlikely and said so in no uncertain tones. We heard more subdued bumpings as he moved around the hull to the air lock, and then there was a long pause while he examined the controls. They're standard on every ship, and there's no way of locking them from outside, so he did not expect much difficulty here.

"It's opening," he announced tersely. "I'm going aboard."

There was another anxious interval. When Peter spoke again, his voice was much fainter, owing to the shielding effect of the ship's hull, but we could still hear him when we turned the volume up.

"The control room looks perfectly normal," he reported, with more than a trace of disappointment in his voice. "We're going to have a look at the cargo."

"It's a little late to mention this," said Tim, "but do you realize that *you're* committing piracy or something very much like it? I suppose the lawyers would call it 'unauthorized entry of a spaceship without the knowledge and consent of the owners.' Anyone know what the penalty is?"

Nobody did, though there were several alarming suggestions. Then Peter called to us again.

"This is a nuisance. The hatch to the stores is locked. I'm afraid we'll have to give up; they'll have taken the keys with them."

"Not necessarily," we heard Karl reply. "You know how often people leave a spare set in case they lose the one they're carrying. They always hide it in what they imagine is a safe place, but you can usually deduce where it is."

"Then go ahead, Sherlock. Is it still all clear at your end?"

"Yes. The game's nowhere near finished. They seem to have settled down for the afternoon."

To everyone's surprise, Karl found the keys in less than ten minutes. They had been tucked into a little recess under the instrument panel.

"Here we go!" shouted Peter gleefully.

"For goodness' sake, don't interfere with anything," cautioned Tim, now wishing he'd never allowed the exploit. "Just have a look around and come straight home."

There was no reply; Peter was too busy with the door. We heard the muffled "clank" as he finally got it open and there were scrapings as he slid through the entrance. He was still wearing his space suit, so that he could keep in touch with us over the radio. A moment later we heard him shriek: "Karl! Look at this!"

"What's the fuss?" Karl replied, still as calm as ever. "You nearly blew in my eardrums."

We didn't help matters by shouting our own queries, and it was some time before Tim restored order.

"Stop yelling, everybody! Now, Peter, tell us exactly what you've found."

I could hear Peter give a sort of gulp as he collected his breath.

"This ship is full of *guns!*" he gasped. "Honest—I'm not fooling! I can see about twenty of them, clipped to the walls. And they're not like any guns I've ever seen before. They've got funny nozzles, and there are red and green cylinders fixed beneath them. I can't imagine what they're supposed—"

"Karl," Tim demanded, "is Peter pulling our legs?"

"No," came the reply. "It's perfectly true. I don't like to say this, but if there *are* such things as ray guns, we're looking at them now."

"What shall we do?" wailed Peter. He didn't seem happy at finding this support for his theories.

"Don't touch anything!" ordered Tim. "Give us a detailed description of everything you can see and then come straight back."

But before Peter could obey, we all had a second and much worse shock. For suddenly we heard Karl gasp, What's that?"

There was silence for a moment; then a voice I could hardly recognize as Peter's whispered, "There's a ship outside. It's connecting up. What shall we do?"

"Make a run for it," whispered Tim urgently—as if whispering made any difference. "Shoot out of the lock as quickly as you can and come back to the station by different routes. It's dark for another ten minutes; they probably won't see you."

"Too late," said Karl, still hanging on to the last shreds of his composure. "They're already coming aboard. There goes the outer door now."

5 STAR TURN

◆◆

FOR A MOMENT NO ONE could think of anything to say.
Then Tim, still whispering, breathed into the microphone,
"Keep calm! If you tell them that you're in radio contact
with us, they won't dare touch you." This, I couldn't help
thinking, was being rather optimistic. Still, it might be good
for our companions' morale, which was probably at a
pretty low ebb.

"I'm going to grab one of those guns," Peter called. "I
don't know how they work, but it may scare them. Karl,
you take one as well."

"For heaven's sake, be careful!" warned Tim, now
looking very worried. He turned to Ronnie.

"Ron, call the commander and tell him what's happening—quickly! And get a telescope on the *Cygnus* to see
what ship's over there."

We should have thought of this before, of course, but
it had been forgotten in the general excitement.

"They're in the control room now," reported Peter. "I can see them. They're not wearing space suits, and they aren't carrying guns. That gives us quite an advantage."

I suspected that Peter was beginning to feel a little happier, wondering if he might yet be a hero.

"I'm going out to meet them," he announced suddenly. "It's better than waiting in here, where they're bound to find us. Come on, Karl."

We waited breathlessly. I don't know what we expected—anything, I imagine, from a salvo of shots to the hissing or crackling of whatever mysterious weapons our friends were carrying. The one thing we didn't anticipate was what actually happened.

We heard Peter say (and I give him full credit for sounding quite calm): "What are you doing here, and who are you?"

There was silence for what seemed an age. I could picture the scene as clearly as if I'd been present—Peter and Karl standing at bay behind their weapons, the men they had challenged wondering whether to surrender or to make a fight for it.

Then, unbelievably, someone laughed. There were a few words we couldn't catch in what seemed to be English, but they were swept away by a roar of merriment. It sounded as if three or four people were all laughing simultaneously at the tops of their voices.

We could do nothing but wait and wonder until the tumult had finished. Then a new voice, amused and friendly, came from the speaker.

"O.K., boys, you might as well put those gadgets down. You couldn't kill a mouse with them unless you swatted it over the head. I guess you're from the station. If you want to know who we are, this is Twenty-first Century Films, at your service. I'm Lee Thomson, assistant producer. And those ferocious weapons you've got are the ones that Props made for our new interstellar epic. I'm glad to know they've convinced *somebody*. They always looked quite phony to me."

No doubt the reaction had something to do with it, for

we all dissolved in laughter then. When the commander arrived, it was quite a while before anyone could tell him just what had happened.

The funny thing was that, though Peter and Karl had made such fools of themselves, they really had the last laugh. The film people made quite a fuss over them and took them over to their ship, where they had a good deal to eat that wasn't on the station's normal menu.

When we got to the bottom of it, the whole mystery had an absurdly simple explanation. Twenty-first Century were going all out to make a real epic, the first *interstellar* and not merely interplanetary film. And it was going to be the first feature film to be shot entirely in space, without any studio faking.

All this explained the secrecy. As soon as the other companies knew what was going on, they'd all be climbing aboard the bandwagon. Twenty-first Century wanted to get as big a start as possible. They'd shipped up one load of props to await the arrival of the main unit with its cameras and equipment. Besides the "ray guns" that Peter and Karl had encountered, the crates in the hold contained some weird four-legged space suits for the beings that were supposed to live on the planets of Alpha Centauri. Twenty-first Century was doing the thing in style, and we gathered that there was another unit at work on the moon.

The actual shooting was not going to start for another two days, when the actors would be coming up in a third ship. There was much excitement at the news that the star was none other than Linda Lorelli, though we wondered how much of her glamour would be able to get through a space suit. Playing opposite her in one of his usual tough, he-man roles would be Tex Duncan. This was great news to Norman Powell, who had a vast admiration for Tex and had a photograph of him stuck on his locker.

All these preparations next door to us were rather distracting, and whenever we were off duty the station staff would jump into suits and go across to see how the film technicians were getting on. They had to unload their cameras, which were fixed to little rocket units so that they could move around slowly. The second spaceship was now being elaborately disguised by the addition of blisters, turrets and fake gun-housings to make it look (so Twenty-first Century hoped) like a battleship from another solar system. It was really quite impressive.

We were at one of Commander Doyle's lectures when the stars came aboard. The first we knew of their arrival was when the door opened and a small procession drifted in. The Station Commander came first, then his deputy, and then Linda Lorelli. She was wearing a rather worried smile, and it was quite obvious that she found the absence of gravity very confusing. Remembering my own early struggles, I sympathized with her. She was escorted by an elderly woman who seemed at home under zero g and gave Linda a helpful push when she showed signs of being stuck.

Tex Duncan followed close behind. He was trying to manage without an escort and not succeeding very well. He was a good deal older than I'd guessed from his films, probably at least thirty-five. And you could see through his hair in any direction you cared to look. I glanced at Norman, wondering how he'd reacted to the appearance of his hero. He looked just a shade disappointed.

It seemed that everyone had heard about Peter and Karl's adventure, for Miss Lorelli was introduced to them, and they all shook hands very politely. She asked several sensible questions about their work, shuddered at the equations Commander Doyle had written on the blackboard and invited us all across to the company's largest ship, the *Orson Welles*, for tea. I thought she was very nice, much more agreeable than Tex, who looked bored stiff with the whole business.

After this, I'm afraid, the *Morning Star* was deserted, particularly when we found that we could make some money giving a hand on the sets. The fact that we were all used to weightlessness made us very useful, for though most of the film technicians had been into space before, they were not very happy under zero g and so moved slowly and cautiously. We could manage things much more efficiently, once we had been told what to do.

A good deal of the film was being shot on sets inside the *Orson Welles,* which had been fitted up as a sort of flying studio. All the scenes which were supposed to take place inside a spaceship were being shot here against suitable backgrounds of machinery, control boards, and so on. The really interesting sequences, however, were those which had to be filmed out in space.

There was one episode, we gathered, in which Tex Duncan would have to save Miss Lorelli from falling helplessly through space into the path of an approaching planet. As it was one of Twenty-first Century's proudest boasts that Tex never used stand-ins, but actually carried out even the most dangerous feats himself, we were all looking forward to this. We thought it might be worth seeing, and as it turned out we were right.

I had now been on the station for a fortnight and considered myself an old hand. It seemed perfectly natural to have no weight, and I had almost forgotten the meaning of the words "up" and "down." Such matters as sucking liquids through tubes instead of drinking them from cups or glasses were no longer novelties but part of everyday life.

I think there was only one thing I really missed on the station. It was impossible to have a bath the way you could on earth. I'm very fond of lying in a hot tub until someone comes banging on the door to make certain I haven't fallen asleep. On the station you could have only a shower, and even this meant standing inside a fabric cylinder and lacing it tight round your neck to prevent the spray from escaping. Any large volume of water formed a big globe that would float around until it hit a wall. When that happened, some of it would break up into smaller drops which would go wandering off on their own, but most of it would spread all over the surface it had touched, making a horrid mess.

Over in the Residential Station, where there was gravity, they had baths and even a small swimming pool. Everyone thought that this last idea was simply showing off.

The rest of the staff, as well as the apprentices, had come to take me for granted and sometimes I was able to help in odd jobs. I'd learned as much as I could, without bothering people by asking too many questions, and had filled four thick notebooks with information and sketches. When I got back to earth, I'd be able to write a book about the station if I wanted to.

As long as I kept in touch with Tim Benton or the commander, I was now allowed to go more or less where I liked. The place that fascinated me most was the observatory, where they had a small but powerful telescope that I could play with when no one else was using it.

I never grew tired of looking at the earth as it waxed and waned below. Usually the countries beneath us were clear of cloud, and I could get distinct views of the lands over which we were hurtling. Because of our speed, the ground beneath was rolling back five miles every second. But as we were five hundred miles up, if the telescope was kept tracking correctly you could keep an object in the field of view for quite a long time, before it got lost in the mists near the horizon. There was a neat automatic gadget on the telescope mounting that took care of this. Once you'd set the instrument on anything, it kept swinging at just the right speed.

As we swept around the world, I could survey in each hundred minutes a belt stretching as far north as Japan, the Gulf of Mexico and the Red Sea. To the south I could see as far as Rio de Janeiro, Madagascar and Australia. It was a wonderful way of learning geography, though because of the earth's curvature the more distant countries were very much distorted, and it was hard to recognize them from ordinary maps.

Lying as it did above the Equator, the orbit of the

station passed directly above two of the world's greatest rivers, the Congo and the Amazon. With my telescope I could see right into the jungles and had no difficulty at all in picking out individual trees and the larger animals. The great African Reservation was a wonderful place to watch, because if I hunted around I could find almost any animal I cared to name.

I also spent a lot of time looking outward, away from earth. Although I was virtually no nearer the moon and planets than I was on earth—for at this altitude I was still only a five-hundredth of the way to the moon—now that I was outside the atmosphere I could get infinitely clearer views. The great lunar mountains seemed so close that I wanted to reach out and run my fingers along their ragged crests. Where it was night on the moon I could see some of the lunar colonies shining away like stars in the darkness. But the most wonderful sight of all was the take-off of a spaceship. When I had a chance, I'd listen to the radio and make a note of departure times. Then I'd go to the telescope, aim it at the right part of the moon, and wait.

All I'd see at first would be a circle of darkness. Suddenly there'd be a tiny spark that would grow brighter and brighter. At the same time it would begin to expand as the rocket rose higher and the glare of its exhausts lit up more and more of the lunar landscape. In that brilliant, blue-white illumination I could see the mountains and plains of the moon, shining as brightly as they ever did in daylight. As the rocket climbed, the circle of light would grow wider and fainter, until presently it was too dim to reveal any more details of the land beneath. The ascending spaceship would become a brilliant, tiny star moving swiftly across the moon's dark face. A few minutes later, the star would wink out of existence almost as suddenly as it had been born. The ship had escaped from the moon and was safely launched on its journey. In thirty or forty hours it would be sweeping into the orbit of the station, and I would be watching its crew come aboard, as unconcernedly as if they'd just taken a 'copter ride to the next town.

I think I wrote more letters while I was on the station than I did in a year at home. They were all very short, and they all ended: "P.S. Please send this cover back to me for my collection." That was one way of making sure I'd have a set of space-mail stamps that would be the envy of everyone in our district. I stopped when I ran out of money, and a lot of distant aunts and uncles were probably surprised to hear from me.

I also did one TV interview, a two-way affair, with my questioner down on earth. It seems there'd been a good deal of interest roused by my trip to the station, and everyone wanted to know how I was getting on. I told them I was having a fine time and didn't want to come back for a while, at any rate. There were still plenty of things to do and see, and the Twenty-first Century film unit was now getting into its stride.

While the technicians were making their preparations, Tex Duncan had been learning how to use a space suit. One of the engineers had the job of teaching him, and we learned that he didn't think much of his pupil. Mr. Duncan was too sure that he knew all the answers, and because he could fly a jet he thought handling a suit would be easy.

I got a ringside seat the day they started the freespace shots. The unit was operating about fifty miles away from the station, and we'd gone over in the *Skylark,* our private yacht, as we sometimes called her.

Twenty-first Century had had to make this move for a rather amusing reason. One would have thought that, since they had at great trouble and expense got their actors and cameras out into space, they had only to go ahead and start shooting. But they soon found that it didn't work out that way. For one thing, the lighting was all wrong.

Above the atmosphere, when you're in direct sunshine, it's as if you have a single, intense spotlight playing on you. The sunward side of any object is brilliantly illuminated, the dark side utterly black. As a result, when you look at an object in space you can see only part of it. You may have to wait until it's revolved and been fully illuminated before you can get a picture of it as a whole.

One gets used to this sort of thing in time, but Twenty-first Century decided that it would upset audiences down on earth. So they decided to get some additional lighting to fill in the shadows. For a while they even considered dragging out extra floodlights and floating them in space around the actors, but the power needed to compete with the sun was so tremendous that they gave up the idea. Then someone said, "Why not use mirrors?" This idea would probably have fallen through as well, if somebody else hadn't remembered that the biggest mirror ever built was floating in space only a few miles away.

The old solar power station had been out of use for over thirty years, but its giant reflector was still as good as new. It had been built in the early days of astronautics to tap the flood of energy pouring from the sun, and to convert it into useful electric power. The main reflector was a great bowl almost three hundred feet across, shaped just like a searchlight mirror. Sunlight falling upon it was concentrated onto heating coils at the focus, where it flashed water into steam and so drove turbines and generators.

The mirror itself was a very flimsy structure of curved girders, supporting incredibly thin sheets of metallic sodium. Sodium had been used because it was light and formed a good reflector. All these thousands of facets collected the sunlight and beamed it at one spot, where the heating coils had been when the station was operating. However, the generating gear had been removed long ago, and only the great mirror was left, floating aimlessly in space. No one minded Twenty-first Century using it for their own purposes if they wanted to. They asked permission, were charged a nominal rent, and told to go ahead.

What happened then was one of those things that seems very obvious afterward, but which nobody thinks of beforehand. When we arrived on the scene, the camera crews were in place about five hundred feet from the great mirror, some distance off the line between it and the sun. Anything on this line was now illuminated on both sides—from one direction by direct sunlight, from the other by light which had fallen on the mirror, been brought to a focus, and spread out again. I'm sorry if this all sounds a bit complicated, but it's important that you understand the setup.

The *Orson Welles* was floating behind the cameramen, who were playing round with a dummy to get the right angles when we arrived. When everything was perfect, the dummy would be hauled in and Tex Duncan would take its place. Everyone would have to work quickly because they wanted the crescent earth in the background. Unfortunately, because of our swift orbital movement, earth waxed and waned so quickly that only ten minutes in every hour were suitable for filming.

While these preparations were being made, we went in the power station control room. This was a large pressurized cylinder on the rim of the great mirror, with windows giving a good view in all directions. It had been made habitable and the air-conditioning brought into service again by some of our own technicians—for a suitable fee, of course. They had also had the job of swinging the mirror round until it faced the sun once more. This had been done by fixing some rocket units to the rim and letting them fire for a few seconds at the calculated times. Quite a tricky business, and one that could be done only by experts.

We were rather surprised to find Commander Doyle in the sparsely furnished control room. For his part, he seemed a little embarrassed to meet us. I wondered why he was interested in earning some extra money since he never went down to earth to spend it.

While we were waiting for something to happen, he explained how the station had operated and why the development of cheap and simple atomic generators had made the place obsolete. From time to time I glanced out of the window to see how the cameramen were getting on. We had a radio tuned in to their circuit, and the director's instructions came over it in a never-ending stream. I'm sure he wished he was back in a studio down on earth, and was

cursing whoever had thought of this crazy idea of shooting a film in space.

The great concave mirror was a really impressive sight
from here on its rim. A few of the facets were missing,
and I could see the stars shining through, but apart from
this it was quite intact—and, of course, completely untarnished. I felt like a fly crawling on the edge of a metal
saucer. Although the entire bowl of the mirror was being
flooded with sunlight, it seemed dark from where we
were stationed. All the light it was collecting was going to a
point about two hundred feet out in space. There were
still some supporting girders reaching out to the focus point
where the heating coils had been, but now they simply
ended in nothingness.

The great moment arrived at last. We saw the air lock
of the *Orson Welles* swing open and Tex Duncan emerged.
He had learned to handle his space suit reasonably well,
though I'm sure I could have done better if I'd had as
much chance to practice.

The dummy was pulled away, the director started giving
his instructions, and the cameras began to follow Tex.
There was little for him to do in this scene except to make
a few simple maneuvers with his suit. He was, I gathered,
supposed to be adrift in space after the destruction of his
ship and was trying to locate any other survivors. Needless
to say, Miss Lorelli would be among them, but she hadn't
yet appeared on the scene. Tex held the stage—if you
could call it that—all to himself.

The cameras continued shooting until the earth was half
full and some of the continents had become recognizable.
There was no point in continuing then, for this would give
the game away. The action was supposed to be taking place
off one of the planets of Alpha Centauri, and it would
never do if the audience recognized New Guinea, India or
the Gulf of Mexico. That would destroy the illusion with a
bang.

There was nothing to do but wait for thirty minutes until earth became a crescent again, and its telltale geography
was hidden by mist or cloud. We heard the director tell the

camera crews to stop shooting, and everyone relaxed. Tex announced over the radio, "I'm lighting a cigarette—I've always wanted to smoke in a space suit." Somebody behind me muttered, "Showing off again—serve him right if it makes him spacesick!"

There were a few more instructions to the camera crews, and then we heard Tex again.

"Another twenty minutes, did you say? Darned if I'll hang round all that time. I'm going over to look at this glorified shaving mirror."

"That means *us*," remarked Tim Benton in deep disgust.

"O.K.," replied the director, who probably knew better than to argue with Tex. "But be sure you're back in time."

I was watching through the observation port and saw the faint mist from Tex's jets as he started toward us.

"He's going pretty fast," someone remarked. "I hope he can stop in time. We don't want any more holes in our nice mirror."

Then everything seemed to happen at once. I heard Commander Doyle shouting, "Tell that fool to stop! Tell him to brake for all he's worth! He's heading for the focus —it'll burn him to a cinder!"

It was several seconds before I understood what he meant. Then I remembered that all the light and heat collected by our great mirror was being poured into that tiny volume of space toward which Tex was blissfully floating. Someone had told me that it was equal to the heat of ten thousand electric fires, and concentrated into a beam only a few feet wide. Yet there was absolutely nothing visible to the eye, no way in which one could sense the danger until it was too late. Beyond the focus, the beam spread out again, soon to become harmless. But where the heating coils had been, in that gap between the girders, it could melt any metal in seconds. Tex had aimed himself straight at the gap! If he reached it, he would last about as long as a moth in an oxyacetylene flame!

6   HOSPITAL IN SPACE

◆◆◆

SOMEONE WAS SHOUTING OVER the radio, trying to send a warning to Tex. Even if it reached him in time, I wondered if he'd have sense enough to act correctly. It was just as likely that he'd panic and start spinning out of control without altering his course.

The commander must have realized this, for suddenly he shouted:

"Hold tight, everybody! I'm going to tip the mirror!"

I grabbed the nearest handhold. Commander Doyle, with a single jerk of those massive forearms, launched himself across to the temporary control panel that had been installed near the observation window. He glanced up at the approaching figure and did some rapid mental calculations. Then his fingers flashed out and played across the switches of the rocket firing panel.

Three hundred feet away, on the far side of the great mirror, I saw the first jets of flame stabbing against the stars. A shudder ran through the framework all around us; it was never meant to be swung as quickly as this. Even so, it seemed to turn very slowly. Then I saw that the sun was moving off to one side. We were no longer aimed directly toward it, and the invisible cone of fire converging from our mirror was now opening out harmlessly into space. How near it passed to Tex we never knew, but he said later that there was one brief, blinding explosion of light that swept past him, leaving him blinded for minutes.

The controlling rockets burned themselves out, and with a gasp of relief I let go of my handhold. Although the acceleration had been slight (there was not enough power in these small units to produce any really violent effect), it was more than the mirror had ever been designed to withstand, and some of the reflecting surfaces had torn adrift and were slowly spinning in space. So, for that matter, was the whole power station. It would take a long period of careful juggling with the jets to iron out the spin that Commander Doyle had given it. Sun, earth and stars were slowly turning all about us and I had to close my eyes before I could get any sense of orientation.

When I opened them again, the commander was busily talking to the *Orson Welles*, explaining just what had happened and saying exactly what he thought of Mr. Duncan. That was the end of shooting for the day, and it was quite a while before anyone saw Tex again.

Soon after this episode, our visitors packed their things and went farther out into space, much to our disappointment. The fact that we were in darkness for half the time, while passing through the shadow of the earth, was too big a handicap for efficient filming. Apparently they had never thought of this, and when we heard of them again they were ten thousand miles out, in a slightly tilted orbit that kept them in perpetual sunlight.

We were sorry to see them go, because they had provided much entertainment and we'd been anxious to see the famous ray guns in action. To everyone's surprise, the entire unit eventually got back to earth safely. But we're still waiting for the film to appear.

It was the end, too, of Norman's hero worship. The photo of Tex vanished from his locker and was never seen again.

In my prowling around, I'd now visited almost every part of the station that wasn't strictly out of bounds. The forbidden territory included the power plant—which was radioactive anyway, so that nobody could go into it—the Stores Section, guarded by a fierce quartermaster, and the main control room. This was one place I'd badly wanted to go; it was the "brain" of the station, from which radio contact was maintained with all the ships in this section of space, and of course with earth itself. Until everyone knew that I could be trusted not to make a nuisance of myself, there was little chance of my being allowed in there. But I was determined to manage it someday, and at last I got the opportunity.

One of the tasks of the junior apprentices was to take coffee and light refreshments to the duty officer in the middle of his watch. This always occurred when the station was crossing the Greenwich Meridian. Since it took exactly a hundred minutes for us to make one trip around the earth, everything was based on this interval and our clocks were adjusted to give a local "hour" of this length. After a while one got used to being able to judge the time simply by glancing at the earth and seeing what continent was beneath.

The coffee, like all drinks, was carried in closed containers (nicknamed "milk bottles") and had to be drunk by sucking through a plastic tube, since it wouldn't pour in the absence of gravity. The refreshments were taken up to the control room in a light frame with little holes for the various containers, and their arrival was always much appreciated by the staff on duty, except when they were dealing with some emergency and were too busy for anything else.

It took a lot of persuading before I got Tim Benton to put me down for this job. I pointed out that it relieved the other boys for more important work; to which he retorted that it was one of the few jobs they *liked* doing. But at last he gave in.

I'd been carefully briefed, and just as the station was passing over the Gulf of Guinea I stood outside the control room and tinkled my little bell. (There were a lot of quaint customs like this aboard the station.) The duty officer shouted, "Come in!" I steered my tray through the door and then handed out the food and drinks. The last milk bottle reached its customer just as we were passing over the African coast.

They must have known I was coming because no one seemed in the least surprised to see me. As I had to stay and collect the empties, there was plenty of opportunity to look around the control room. It was spotlessly clean and tidy, dome-shaped, and with a wide glass panel running right round it. Besides the duty officer and his assistant, there were several radio operators at their instruments, and other men working on equipment I couldn't recognize. Dials and TV screens were everywhere, lights were flashing on and off, yet the whole place was silent. The men sitting at their little desks were wearing headphones and throat microphones, so that any two people could talk without disturbing the others. It was fascinating to watch these experts working swiftly at their tasks, directing ships thousands of miles away, talking to the other space stations or to the moon and checking the many instruments on which our lives depended.

The duty officer sat at a huge glass-topped desk on which glowed a complicated pattern of colored lights. It showed the earth, the orbits of the other stations and the courses of all the ships in our part of space. From time to time he would say something quietly, his lips scarcely moving, and I knew that some order was winging its way out to an approaching ship, telling it to hold off a little longer or to prepare for contact.

I dared not hang around once I'd finished my job, but the next day I had a second chance. Because things were rather slack, one of the assistants was kind enough to show me around. He let me listen to some of the radio conversations, and explained the workings of the great display panel. The thing that impressed me most of all, however, was the shining metal cylinder, covered with controls and winking lights, which occupied the center of the room.

"This," said my guide proudly, "is HAVOC."

"What?" I asked.

"Short for *A*utomatic *V*oyage *O*rbit *C*omputer."

I thought this over for a moment.

"What does the *H* stand for?"

"Everyone asks that. It doesn't stand for anything." He turned to the operator.

"What's she set up for now?"

The man gave an answer that consisted chiefly of mathematics, but I did catch the word "Venus."

"Right. Let's suppose we wanted to leave for Venus in—oh, four hours from now." His hands flicked across a keyboard like that of an overgrown typewriter.

I expected HAVOC to whir and click, but all that happened was that a few lights changed color. Then, after about ten seconds, a buzzer sounded twice and a piece of tape slid out of a narrow slot. It was covered with closely printed figures.

"There you are—everything you want to know. Direction of firing, elements of orbit, time of flight, when to start braking. All you need now is a spaceship!"

I wondered just how many hundreds of calculations the electronic brain had carried out in those few seconds. Space travel was certainly a complicated affair, so complicated that it sometimes depressed me. Then I remembered that these men didn't seem any cleverer than I was; they were highly trained, that was all. If one worked hard enough, one could master anything.

My time on the Inner Station was now drawing to an end, though not in the way anyone had expected. I had slipped into the uneventful routine of life, and it had been explained to me that nothing exciting ever happened up here and if I'd wanted thrills I should have stayed back on earth. That was a little disappointing, for I'd hoped that something out of the ordinary would take place while I was here, though I couldn't imagine what. As it turned out, my wish was soon to be fulfilled.

But before I come to that, I see I'll have to say something about the other space stations, which I've neglected so far.

Ours, only five hundred miles up, was the nearest to the earth, but there were others doing equally important jobs at much greater distances. The farther out they were, the longer, of course, they took to make a complete revolution. Our "day" was only a hundred minutes, but the outermost stations of all took twenty-four hours to complete their orbit, thus providing the curious results which I'll mention later.

The purpose of the Inner Station, as I've explained, was to act as a refueling, repair and transfer point for spaceships, both outgoing and incoming. For this job, it was necessary to be as close to the earth as possible. Much lower than five hundred miles would not have been safe since the last faint traces of air would have robbed the station of its speed and eventually brought it crashing down.

The Meteorological Stations, on the other hand, had to be a fair distance out so that they could "see" as much of the earth as possible. There were two of them, six thousand miles up, circling the world every six and a half hours. Like our Inner Station, they moved over the Equator. This meant that, though they could see much farther north and south than we could, the polar regions were still out of sight or badly distorted. Hence the existence of the Polar Met Station, which, unlike all the others, had an orbit passing over the poles. Together, the three stations could get a practically continuous picture of the weather over the whole planet.

A good deal of astronomical work was also carried on in these stations. Some very large telescopes had been constructed here, floating in free orbit where their weight wouldn't matter.

Beyond the Met Stations, fifteen thousand miles up, circled the biology labs and the famous Space Hospital. There a great deal of research into zero-gravity conditions was carried out, and many diseases which were incurable on earth could be treated. For example, the heart no longer had to work so hard to pump blood round the body, and so could be rested in a manner impossible on earth.

Finally, twenty-two thousand miles out were the three great Relay Stations. They took exactly a day to make one revolution; therefore they appeared to be fixed forever over the same spots on the earth. Linked to each other by tight radio beams, they provided TV coverage over the whole planet. And not only TV, but all the long-distance radio and 'phone services passed through the Relay Chain, the building of which at the close of the twentieth century had completely revolutionized world communications.

One station, serving the Americas, was in Latitude 90° West. A second, in 30° East, covered Europe and Africa. The third, in 150° East, served the entire Pacific area. There was no spot on earth where you could not pick up one or other of the stations. And once you had trained your receiving equipment in the right direction, there was never any need to move it again. The sun, moon and planets might rise and set, but the three Relay Stations never moved from their fixed positions in the sky.

The different orbits were connected by a shuttle service of small rockets which made trips at infrequent intervals. On the whole, there was little traffic between the various stations. Most of their business was done directly with earth. At first I had hoped to visit some of our neighbors, but a few inquiries had made it obvious that I hadn't a chance. I was due to return home inside a week, and there was no spare passenger space available during that time. Even if there had been, it was pointed out to me, there were many more useful loads that could be carried.

I was in the *Morning Star* watching Ronnie Jordan put the finishing touches to a beautiful model spaceship when the radio called. It was Tim Benton, on duty back at the station. He sounded very excited.

"Is that Ron? Anyone else there—what, only Roy? Well, never mind—listen to this, it's very important."

"Go ahead," replied Ron. We were both considerably surprised, for we'd never heard Tim really excited before.

"We want to use the *Morning Star*. I've promised the commander that she'll be ready in three hours."

"What!" gasped Ronnie. "I don't believe it!"

"There's no time to argue—I'll explain later. The others are coming over right away. They'll have to use space suits, as you've got the *Skylark* with you. Now then, make a list of these points and start checking."

For the next twenty minutes we were busy testing the controls—that is, those which would operate at all. We couldn't imagine what had happened, but were too fully occupied to do much speculating. Fortunately, I'd got to know my way around the *Morning Star* so thoroughly that I was able to give Ron quite a bit of help, calling meter readings to him, and so on.

Presently there was a bumping and banging from the air lock and three of our colleagues came aboard, towing batteries and power tools. They had made the trip on one of the rocket tractors used for moving ships and stores around the station, and had brought two drums of fuel across with them, enough to fill the auxiliary tanks. From them we discovered what all the fuss was about.

It was a medical emergency. One of the passengers from a Mars-Earth liner, which had just docked at the Residential Station, had been taken seriously ill and had to have an operation within ten hours. The only chance of saving his life was to get him out to the Space Hospital, but unfortunately ships at the Inner Station were being serviced and would take at least a day to get spaceworthy.

It was Tim who'd talked the commander into giving us this chance. The *Morning Star,* he pointed out, had been very carefully looked after, and the requirements for a trip to the Space Hospital were not great. Only a small amount of fuel would be needed, and it wouldn't even be necessary to use the main motors. The whole journey could be made on the auxiliary rockets.

Since he could think of no alternative, Commander Doyle had reluctantly agreed, after stating a number of conditions. We had to get the *Morning Star* over to the station under her own power so that she could be fueled up and *he* would do all the piloting.

During the next hour, I did my best to be useful and to become accepted as one of the crew. My chief job was going over the ship and securing loose objects, which might start crashing round when power was applied. Perhaps "crashing" is too strong a word, as we weren't going to use much of an acceleration. But anything adrift might be a nuisance and could even be dangerous if it got into the wrong place.

It was a great moment when Norman Powell started the motors. He gave a short burst of power at very low thrust, while everyone watched the meters for signs of danger. We were all wearing our space suits as a safety precaution. If one of the motors exploded, it would probably not harm us up here in the control room, but it might easily spring a leak in the hull.

Everything went according to plan. The mild acceleration made us all drift toward what had suddenly become the floor. Then the feeling of weight ceased again, and everything was normal once more.

There was much comparing of meter readings, and at last Norman said, "the motors seem O.K. Let's get started."

And so the *Morning Star* began her first voyage for almost a hundred years. It was not much of a journey, compared with her great trip to Venus. In fact, it was only about five miles, from the graveyard over to the Inner Station. Yet to all of us it was a real adventure, for we were all very fond of the wonderful old ship.

We reached the Inner Station after about five minutes, and Norman brought the ship to rest several hundred yards away. He was taking no risks with his first command. The tractors were already fussing around, and before long the towropes had been attached and the *Morning Star* was hauled in.

It was at that point that I decided I'd better keep out of the way. Rear of the workshop (which had once been the *Morning Star*'s hold) were several smaller chambers, usually occupied by stores. Most of the loose equipment aboard the ship had now been stuffed into these and lashed securely in place. However, there was still plenty of room left.

I want to make one thing quite clear. Although the word "stowaway" has been used, I don't consider it at all accurate. No one had actually told me to leave the ship, and I wasn't hiding. If anybody had come through the workshop and rummaged around in the storeroom, he would have seen me. But nobody did, so whose fault was that?

Time seemed to go very slowly while I waited. I could hear distant, muffled shouts and orders, and after a while there came the unmistakable pulsing of the pumps as fuel came surging into the tanks. Then there was another long interval. I knew Commander Doyle must be waiting until the ship had reached the right point in her orbit around the earth before he turned on the motors. I had no idea when this would be, and the suspense was terrible.

But at last the rockets roared into life. Weight returned. I slid down the walls and found myself really standing on a solid floor again. I took a few steps to see what it felt like and didn't enjoy the experience. In the last fortnight I had grown so accustomed to lack of gravity that its temporary return was a nuisance.

The thunder of the motors lasted for three or four minutes, and by the end of that time I was almost deafened by the noise, though I had pushed my fingers into my ears. Passengers weren't supposed to travel so near the rockets, and I was very glad when at last there was a sudden slackening in thrust and the roar surrounding me began to fade. Soon it ebbed into silence, though my head was still ringing, and it would be quite a while before I could hear properly again. But I didn't mind that. All that really mattered was that the journey had begun, and no one could send me back!

I decided to wait for a while before going up to the control room. Commander Doyle would still be busy checking his course, and I didn't want to bother him while he was occupied. Besides, I had to think of a good story.

Everyone was surprised to see me. There was complete silence when I drifted through the door and said: "Hello! I think someone might have warned me that we were going to take off."

Commander Doyle simply stared at me. For a moment I couldn't decide whether he was going to be angry or not. Then he said: "What are *you* doing aboard?"

"I was lashing down the gear in the storeroom."

He turned to Norman, who looked a little unhappy. "Is that correct?"

"Yes, sir. I told him to do it, but I thought he'd finished."

The commander considered this for a moment. Then he said to me: "Well, we've no time to go into this now. You're here, and we'll have to put up with you."

This was not very flattering, but it might have been much worse. And the expression on Norman's face was worth going a long way to see.

The remainder of the *Morning Star*'s crew consisted of Tim Benton, who was looking at me with a quizzical smile, and Ronnie Jordan, who avoided my gaze altogether. We had two passengers. The sick man was strapped to a stretcher that had been fixed against one wall; he must have been drugged, for he remained unconscious for the whole journey. With him was a young doctor who did nothing except look anxiously at his watch and give his patient an injection from time to time. I don't think he said more than a dozen words during the whole trip.

Tim explained to me later that the sick man was suffering from an acute, and fortunately very rare, type of stomach trouble caused by the return of high gravity. It was very lucky for him that he had managed to reach the earth's orbit, because if he had been taken ill on the two months' voyage, the medical resources of the liner could not have saved him.

There was nothing for any of us to do while the *Morning Star* swept outward on the long curve that would bring her, after some three and a half hours, to the Space Hospital. Very slowly, earth was receding behind us. It was no longer so close that it filled almost half the sky. Already we could see far more of its surface than was possible from the Inner Station, skimming low above the Equator. Northward, the Mediterranean crept into view; then Japan and New Zealand appeared almost simultaneously over opposite horizons.

And still the earth dwindled behind us. Now it was a sphere at last, hanging out there in space, small enough for the eye to take in the whole of it at one glance. I could now see so far to the south that the great Antarctic ice cap was just visible, a gleaming white fringe beyond the tip of Patagonia.

We were fifteen thousand miles above the earth, swimming into the path of the Space Hospital. In a moment we would have to use the rockets again to match orbits. This time, however, I should have a more comfortable ride, here in the soundproof cabin.

Once again weight returned with the roaring rockets. There was one prolonged burst of power, then a series of short corrections. When it was all over, Commander Doyle unstrapped himself from the pilot's seat and drifted over to the observation port. His instruments told him where he was far more accurately than his eyes could ever do, but he wanted the satisfaction of seeing for himself. I also made for a port that no one else was using.

Floating there in space beside us was what seemed to be a great crystal flower, its face turned full toward the sun. At first there was no way in which I could judge its true scale or guess how far away it was. Then, through the transparent walls, I could see little figures moving around and catch the gleam of sunlight on complex machines and equipment. The station must be at least five hundred feet in diameter, and the cost of lifting all this material fifteen thousand miles from the earth must be staggering. Then I recalled that very little of it *had* come from earth, anyway. Like the other stations, the Space Hospital had been constructed almost entirely from components manufactured on the moon.

As we slowly drifted closer, I could see people gathering in the observation decks and glass-roofed wards to watch our arrival. For the first time, it occurred to me that this flight of the *Morning Star* really was something of an event. All the radio and TV networks would be covering it. As a news story, it had everything—a race for life and a gallant effort by a long-retired ship. When we reached the hospital, we would have to run the gantlet.

The rocket tractors came fussing up to us and the tow-ropes started to haul us in. A few minutes later the air locks clamped together, and we were able to go through the connecting tube into the hospital. We waited for the doctor and his still unconscious patient to go first, then went reluctantly forward to meet the crowd waiting to welcome us.

Well, I wouldn't have missed it for anything, and I'm sure the commander enjoyed it as much as any of us. They made a huge fuss and treated us like heroes. Although I hadn't done a thing and really had no right to be there at all (there were some rather awkward questions about that), I was treated just like the others. We were, in fact, given the run of the place.

It seemed that we would have to wait there for two days before we could go back to the Inner Station because there was no earthbound ship until then. Of course, we *could* have made the return trip in the *Morning Star,* but Commander Doyle vetoed this.

"I don't mind tempting providence once," he said, "but I'm not going to do it again. Before the old lady makes another trip, she's going to be overhauled and the motors tested. I don't know if you noticed it, but the combustion chamber temperature was starting to rise unpleasantly while we were doing our final approach. *And* there were about six other things that weren't all they should have been. I'm not going to be a hero twice in one week. The second time might be the last!"

It was, I suppose, a reasonable attitude, but we were a little disappointed. Because of this caution, the *Morning Star* didn't get back to her usual parking place for almost a month, to the great annoyance of her patrons.

Hospitals are, I think, usually slightly depressing places, but this one was different. Few of the patients here were seriously ill, though down on earth most of them would have been dead or completely disabled, owing to the effect of gravity on their weakened hearts. Many were eventually able to return to earth, others could live safely only on the moon or Mars, and the severest cases had to remain permanently on the station. It was a kind of exile, but they seemed cheerful enough. The hospital was a huge place, ablaze with sunshine, and almost everything that could be found on earth was available—everything, that is, that did not depend on gravity.

Only about half of the station was taken up by the hospital; the remainder was devoted to research of various kinds. We were given some interesting conducted tours of the gleaming, spotless labs. And on one of these tours —well, this is what happened.

The commander was away on some business in the Technical Section, but we had been invited to visit the Biology Department, which, we were promised, would be highly interesting. As it turned out, this was an understatement.

We'd been told to meet a Dr. Hawkins on Corridor Nine, Biology Two. Now it's very easy to get lost in a space station—since all the local inhabitants know their way around perfectly, no one bothers with signposts. We found our way to what we thought was Corridor Nine, but couldn't see any door labeled "Biology Two." However, there was a "Biophysics Two," and after some discussion we decided that would be near enough. There would certainly be someone inside who could redirect us.

Tim Benton was in front and opened the door cautiously.

"Can't see a thing," he grumbled. "Phew—it smells like a fishmonger's on a hot day!"

I peered over his shoulder. The light was very dim, and I could make out only a few vague shapes. It was also very warm and moist, with sprays hissing continuously on all sides. There was a peculiar odor that I couldn't identify, a cross between a zoo and a hothouse.

"This place is no good," said Ronnie Jordan in disgust. "Let's try somewhere else."

"Just a minute," exclaimed Norman, whose eyes must have become accustomed to the gloom more quickly than mine. "What do you think! They've got a *tree* in here. At least, it looks like it, though it's a mighty queer one."

He moved forward, and we drifted after him, drawn by the same curiosity. I realized that my companions probably hadn't seen a tree or even a blade of grass for many months. It would be quite a novelty to them.

I could see better now. We were in a very large room, with jars and glass-fronted cages all around us. The air was full of mist from countless sprays, and I felt as if we were in some tropical jungle. There were clusters of lamps all around, but they were turned off and we couldn't see the switches.

About forty feet away was the tree that Norman had noticed. It was certainly an unusual object. A slender, straight trunk rose out of a metal box to which were attached various tubes and pumps. There were no leaves, only a dozen thin, tapering branches drooping straight down, giving it a slightly disconsolate air. It looked like a weeping willow that had been stripped of all its foliage. A continual stream of water played over it from clusters of jets, adding to the general moistness of the air. I was beginning to find it difficult to breathe.

"It can't be from earth," said Tim, "and I've never heard of anything like it on Mars or Venus."

We had now drifted to within a few feet of the object, and the closer we got, the less I liked it. I said so, but Norman only laughed.

His laugh turned to a yell of pure fright. For suddenly that slender trunk leaned toward us, and the long branches shot out like whips. One curled around my ankle, another grasped my waist. I was too scared even to yell. I realized, too late, that this wasn't a tree at all—and that its "branches" were tentacles.

7 WORLD OF MONSTERS

◆◆◆◆◆◆◆◆◆◆◆◆◆◆◆◆◆◆◆◆◆◆◆◆◆◆◆◆◆◆◆◆◆◆◆◆◆◆◆

MY REACTION WAS INSTINCTIVE and violent. Though I was floating in mid-air and so unable to get hold of anything solid, I could still thrash around pretty effectively. The others were doing the same, and presently I came into contact with the floor so that I was able to give a mighty kick. The thin tentacles released their grip as I shot toward the ceiling. I just managed to grasp one of the light fittings in time to stop myself from crashing into the roof, and then looked down to see what had happened to the others.

They had all got clear, and now that my fright was subsiding I realized how feeble those clutching tentacles had really been. If we had been on solid ground with gravity to help us, we could have disengaged ourselves without any trouble. Even here, none of us had been hurt, but we were all badly scared.

"What the devil is it?" gasped Tim when he had recovered his breath and untangled himself from some rub-

ber tubing draped along the wall. Everyone else was too
shaken to answer. We were making our way unsteadily to
the door when there was a sudden flood of light, and
someone called out, "What's all the noise?" A door
opened and a white-smocked man came drifting in. He
stared at us for a moment and said:

"I hope you haven't been teasing Cuthbert."

"Teasing!" spluttered Norman. "I've never had such a
fright in my life. We were looking for Dr. Hawkins and
ran into this—this monster from Mars or whatever it is."

The other chuckled. He launched himself away from
the door and floated toward the now motionless cluster of
tentacles.

"Look out!" cried Tim.

We watched in fascinated horror. As soon as the man
was within range, the slim tendrils struck out again and
whipped round his body. He merely put up an arm to protect his face, but made no other movement to save himself.

"I'm afraid Cuthbert isn't very bright," he said. "He
assumes that anything that comes near him is food and
grabs for it. But we're not very digestible, so he soon lets
go—like this."

The tentacles were already relaxing. With a gesture
exactly like disdain, they thrust away their captive, who
burst out laughing at our startled faces.

"He's not very strong, either. It would be quite easy to
get away from him, even if he wanted to keep you."

"I still don't think it's safe to leave a beast like that
around," said Norman with dignity. "What *is* it, anyway?
Which planet does it come from?"

"You'd be surprised—but I'll let Dr. Hawkins explain
that. He sent me to look for you when you didn't turn up.
And I'm sorry that Cuthbert gave you such a fright. That
door should have been locked, but someone's been careless again."

And that was all the consolation we got. I'm afraid our
mishap had left us in the wrong mood for conducted tours
and scientific explanations, but despite this bad start we
found the Biology Labs quite interesting. Doctor Hawkins,

who was in charge of research here, told us about the work that was going on and about some of the exciting prospects that low gravity had opened up in the way of lengthening the span of life.

"Down on earth," he said, "our hearts have to fight gravity from the moment we're born. Blood is being continually pumped round the body, from head to foot and back again. Only when we're lying down does the heart really get a good rest, and even for the laziest people that's only about a third of their lives. But here, the heart has no work at all to do against gravity."

"Then why doesn't it race, like an engine that has no load?" asked Tim.

"That's a good question. The answer is that nature's provided a wonderful automatic regulator. And there's still quite a bit of work to be done against friction, in the veins and arteries. We don't know yet just what difference zero gravity's going to make, because we haven't been in space long enough. But we think that the expectation of life out here ought to be well over a hundred years. It may even be as much as that on the moon. If we can prove this, it may start all the old folks rushing away from the earth!

"Still, all this is guesswork. Now I'm going to show you something which I think is just as exciting."

He had led us into a room whose walls consisted almost entirely of glass cages, full of creatures which at first sight I could not identify. Then I gave a gasp of astonishment.

"They're flies! But where did they come from?"

They were flies, all right. Only one thing was wrong—these flies had a wing span of a foot or more.

Doctor Hawkins chuckled.

"Lack of gravity, again, plus a few special hormones. Down on earth, you know, an animal's weight has a major effect on controlling its size. A fly this size couldn't possibly lift itself into the air. It's odd to watch these flying; you can see the wing beats quite easily."

"What kind of flies are they?" asked Tim.

"Drosophila—fruit flies. They breed rapidly, and have

been studied on earth for about a century and a half. I can trace this fellow's family tree back to around 1920!"

Personally, I could think of much more exciting occupations, but presumably the biologists knew what they were doing. Certainly the final result was highly impressive—and unpleasant. Flies aren't pretty creatures, even when normal size.

"Now here's a bit of a contrast," said Dr. Hawkins, making some adjustments to a large projection microscope. "You can just about see this chap with the naked eye—in the ordinary way, that is."

He flicked a switch, and a circle of light flashed on the screen. We were looking into a tiny drop of water, with strange blobs of jelly and minute living creatures drifting through the field of vision. And there in the center of the picture, waving its tentacles lazily, was . . .

"Why," exclaimed Ron, "that's like the creature that caught us."

"You're quite right," replied Dr. Hawkins. "It's called a hydra, and a big one is only about a tenth of an inch long. So you see Cuthbert didn't come from Mars or Venus, but was brought from Earth. Increasing his size is our most ambitious experiment yet."

"But what's the idea?" asked Tim.

"Well, you can study these creatures much more easily when they're large. Our knowledge of living matter has been extended enormously since we've been able to do this sort of thing. I must admit, though, that we rather overdid it with Cuthbert. It takes a lot of effort to keep him alive, and we're not likely to try and beat this record."

After that, we were taken to see Cuthbert again. The lights were switched on this time; it seemed that we'd stumbled into the lab during one of the short periods of artificial "night." Though we knew that the creature was safe, we wouldn't go very close. Tim Benton, however, was persuaded to offer a piece of raw meat, which was grabbed by a slim tentacle and tucked into the top of the long, slender "trunk."

"I should have explained," said Dr. Hawkins, "that

hydras normally paralyze their victims by stinging them. There are poison buds all along those tentacles, but we've been able to neutralize them. Otherwise, Cuthbert would be as dangerous as a cageful of cobras."

I felt like saying I didn't really think much of their taste in pets, but I remembered in time that we were guests.

Another high light of our stay at the hospital was the visit to the Gravity Section. I've already mentioned that some of the space stations produce a kind of artificial gravity by spinning slowly on their axes. Inside the hospital they had a huge drum, or centrifuge, that did the same thing. We were given a ride in it, partly for fun and partly as a serious test of our reactions to having weight again.

The gravity chamber was a cylinder about fifty feet in diameter, supported on pivots at either end and driven by electric motors. We entered through a hatch in the side and found ourselves in a small room that would have seemed perfectly normal down on earth. There were pictures hanging from the walls, and even an electric light fixture suspended from the "ceiling." Everything had been done to create an impression, as far as the eye was concerned, that "up" and "down" existed again.

We sat in the comfortable chairs and waited. Presently there was a gentle vibration and a sense of movement: the chamber was beginning to turn. Very slowly, a feeling of heaviness began to steal over me. My legs and arms required an effort to move them: I was a slave of gravity again, no longer able to glide through the air as freely as a bird. . . .

A concealed loud-speaker gave us our instructions. "We'll hold the speed constant now. Get up and walk around—but be careful."

I rose from my seat and almost fell back again with the effort.

"Wow!" I exclaimed. "How much weight have they given us? I feel as if I'm on Jupiter!"

My words must have been picked up by the operator, because the loud-speaker gave a chuckle.

"You're just half the weight you were back on earth.

But it seems considerable, doesn't it, after you've had none at all for a couple of weeks!"

It was a thought that made me feel rather unhappy. When I got down to earth again, I'd weigh twice as much as this! Our instructor must have guessed my thoughts.

"No need to worry. You get used to it quickly enough on the way out, and it will be the same on the way back. You'll just have to take things easy for a few days when you get down to earth, and try and remember that you can't jump out of top-floor windows and float gently to the ground."

Put that way, it sounded silly, but this was just the sort of thing I'd grown accustomed to doing here. I wondered how many spacemen broke their necks when they got back to earth!

In the centrifuge, we tried out all the tricks that were impossible under zero gravity. It was funny to watch liquids pour in a thin stream and remain quietly at the bottom of a glass. I kept on making little jumps, just for the novel experience of coming down quickly again in the same place.

Finally we were ordered back to our seats, the brakes were put on, and the spin of the chamber was stopped. We were weightless again—back to normal!

I wish we could have stayed in the Hospital Station for a week or so, in order to explore the place thoroughly. It had everything that the Inner Station lacked, and my companions, who hadn't been to earth for months, appreciated the luxury even more than I did. It was strange seeing shops and gardens and even going to the theater. *That* was an unforgettable experience. Thanks to the absence of gravity, one could pack a large audience into a small space and everyone could get a good view. But it created a very difficult problem for the producer, as he had to give an illusion of gravity somehow. It wouldn't do in a Shakespeare play for all the characters to be floating around in mid-air. So the actors had to use magnetic shoes —a favorite dodge of the old science fiction writers, though this was the only time I ever found them used in reality.

The play we saw was *Macbeth*. Personally, I don't care for Shakespeare and I went along only because we'd been invited and it would have been rude to stay away. But I was glad I went, if only because it was interesting to see how the patients were enjoying themselves. And not many people can claim that they've seen Lady Macbeth, in the sleepwalking scene, coming down the stairs with magnetic shoes!

Another reason why I was in no great hurry to return to the Inner Station was simply this—in three days' time I'd have to go aboard the freighter scheduled to take me home. Although I'd been mighty lucky to get out here to the Space Hospital, there were still many things I hadn't seen There were the Met Stations, the great observatories with their huge, floating telescopes and the Relay Stations, an other seven thousand miles farther out into space. Well, they would simply have to wait for another time.

Before the ferry rocket arrived to take us home, we had the satisfaction of knowing that our mission had been successful. The patient was off the danger list, and had a good chance of making a complete recovery. But—and this certainly gave the whole thing an ironic twist—it wouldn't be safe for him to go down to earth. He'd come all these scores of millions of miles for nothing. The best he could do would be to look down on earth through observation telescopes, watching the green fields on which he could never walk again. When his convalescence was over, he'd have to go back to Mars and its lower gravity.

The ferry rocket that came up to fetch us home had been diverted from its normal run between the Observatory Stations. When we went aboard, Tim Benton was still arguing with the commander. No—arguing wasn't the right word. No one did *that* with Commander Doyle. But he was saying, very wistfully, that it really was a great pity that we couldn't go back in the *Morning Star*. The commander only grinned. "Wait until you see the report of her overhaul," he advised. "Then you may change your mind I bet she needs new tube linings, at the very least. I'll feel a bit happier in a ship that's a hundred years younger!"

Still, as things turned out, I'm pretty sure the commander wished he'd listened to us. . . .

. It was the first time I'd been aboard one of the low-powered inter-orbit ferries, unless one includes our home-built *Skylark of Space* in this category. The control cabin was much like that of any other spaceship, but from the outside the vessel looked very peculiar. It had been built here in space and, of course, had no streamlining or fins. The cabin was roughly egg-shaped, and connected by three open girders to the fuel tanks and rocket motors. Most of the freight was not taken inside the ship, but was simply lashed to what were rather appropriately called the "luggage racks," a series of wiremesh nets supported on struts. For stores that had to be kept under normal pressure, there was a small hold with a second air lock just behind the control cabin. The whole ship had certainly been built for efficiency rather than beauty.

The pilot was waiting for us when we went aboard, and Commander Doyle spent some time discussing our course with him.

"That's not his job," Norman whispered in my ear, "but the old boy's so glad to be out in space again that he can't help it." I was going to say that I thought the commander spent *all* his time in space; then I realized that from some points of view his office aboard the Inner Station wasn't so very different from an office down on earth.

We had nearly an hour before take-off, ample time for all the checks and last-minute adjustments that would be needed. I got into the bunk nearest to the observation port, so that I could look back at the hospital as we dropped away from its orbit and fell down toward earth. It was hard to believe that this great blossom of glass and plastic—floating here in space with the sun pouring into its wards, laboratories and observation decks—was really spinning round the world at eight thousand miles an hour. As I waited for the voyage to begin, I remembered the attempts I'd had to explain the space stations to Mom. Like a lot of people, she could never really understand why they "didn't fall down."

"Look, Mom," I'd said, "they're moving mighty fast, going around the earth in a big circle. And when anything moves like this, you get centrifugal force. It's just the same when you whirl a stone at the end of a string."

"*I* don't whirl stones on the end of strings," said Mom, "and I hope you won't either, at least not indoors."

"I was only giving an example," I had told her. "It's the one they always use at school. Just as the stone can't fly away because of the pull in the string, so a space station has to stay there because of the pull of gravity. Once it's given the right speed, it'll stay there forever without using any power. It can't *lose* speed because there's no air resistance. Of course, the speed's got to be calculated carefully. Near the earth, where gravity's powerful, a station has to move fast to stay up. It's like tying your stone on to a short piece of string; you have to whirl it quickly. But a long way out, where gravity's weaker, the stations can move slowly."

"I thought it was something like that," she replied. "But what worries me is this—suppose one of the stations *did* lose a bit of speed. Wouldn't it come falling down? The whole thing looks dangerous to me. It seems a sort of balancing act. If anything goes wrong . . ."

I hadn't known the answer then, so I'd only been able to say: "Well, the moon doesn't fall down, and it stays up just the same way." It wasn't until I'd got to the Inner Station that I learned the answer, though I should have been able to work it out for myself. If the velocity of a space station *did* drop a bit, it would simply move into a closer orbit. You'd have to carve off quite a lot of its speed before it came dangerously close to earth, and it would take a vast amount of rocket braking to do this. It couldn't possibly happen by accident.

Now I looked at the clock. Another thirty minutes to go. Funny—why do I feel so sleepy now? I had a good rest last night. Perhaps the excitement's been a bit too much. Well, let's just relax and take things easy—there's nothing to do until we reach the Inner Station in four hours' time. Or is it four days? I really can't remember, but, anyway, it isn't important. Nothing is important any more, not even the fact that everything around me is half-hidden in a pink mist. . . .

Then I heard Commander Doyle shouting. He sounded miles away, and though I had an idea that the words he was calling should mean something, I didn't know what it was. They were still ringing vainly in my ears when I blacked out completely: "Emergency Oxygen!"

8   INTO THE ABYSS

❖❖❖❖❖❖❖❖❖❖❖❖❖❖❖❖❖❖❖❖❖❖❖❖❖❖❖❖❖❖❖❖❖

IT WAS ONE OF THOSE PECULIAR dreams when you know you're dreaming and can't do anything about it. Everything that had happened to me in the last few weeks was all muddled up together, as well as flash backs from earlier experiences. Sometimes things were quite the wrong way round. I was down on earth, but weightless, floating like a cloud over valleys and hills. Or else I was up in the Inner Station, but had to struggle against gravity with every movement I made.

The dream ended in nightmare. I was taking a short cut through the Inner Station, using an illegal but widely practiced method that Norman Powell had shown me. Linking the central part of the station with its outlying pressurized chambers are ventilating ducts, wide enough to take a man. The air moves through them at quite a speed, and there are places where one can enter and get a free ride. It's an exciting experience, and you have to know just what you're doing or you may miss the exit and have to buck the air stream to find a way back. Well, in this dream I was riding the air stream and had lost my way. There ahead of me I could see the great blades of the ventilating fan, sucking me down toward them. *And the protecting grille was gone!* In a few seconds I'd be sliced like a side of bacon. . . .

"He's all right," I heard someone say. "He was only out for a minute. Give him another sniff."

A jet of cold gas played over my face, and I tried to jerk my head out of the way. Then I opened my eyes and realized where I was.

"What happened?" I asked, still feeling rather dazed.

Tim Benton was sitting beside me, an oxygen cylinder in his hand. He didn't look in the least upset.

"We're not quite sure," he said. "But it's O.K. now. A change-over valve must have jammed in the oxygen supply when one of the tanks got empty. You were the only one who passed out, and we've managed to clear the trouble by bashing the oxygen distributor with a hammer. Crude, but it usually works. Of course, it will have to be stripped down when we get back, and someone will have to find out why the alarm didn't work."

I still felt rather muzzy and a little ashamed of myself for fainting, though that wasn't the kind of thing anyone could help. And, after all, I *had* acted as a sort of human guinea pig to warn the others. Or perhaps a better analogy would be one of the canaries the old-time miners took with them to test the air underground.

"Does this sort of thing happen very often?" I asked.

"Very seldom," replied Norman Powell. For once he looked serious. "But there are so many gadgets in a spaceship that you've always got to keep on your toes. In a hundred years we haven't got all the bugs out of spaceflight. If it isn't one thing, it's another."

"Don't be so glum, Norman," said Tim. "We've had our share of trouble for this trip. It'll be plain sailing now."

As it turned out, *that* remark was about the most unfortunate that Tim ever made. I'm sure the others never gave him a chance to forget it.

We were now several miles from the hospital, far enough away to avoid our jet doing any damage to it. The pilot had set his controls and was waiting for the calculated moment to start firing, and everyone else was lying down in his bunk. The acceleration would be too weak to be anything of a strain, but we were supposed to keep out of the pilot's way at blast-off and there was simply nowhere else to go.

The motors roared for nearly two minutes. At the end of that time the hospital was a tiny, brilliant toy twenty or thirty miles away. If the pilot had done his job properly, we were now dropping down on a long curve that would take us back to the Inner Station. We had nothing to do but sit and wait for the next three and a half hours, while the earth grew bigger and bigger until it once more filled almost half the sky.

On the way out, because of our patient we hadn't been able to talk, but there was nothing to stop us now. There was a curious kind of elation, even lightheadedness, about our little party. If I'd stopped to think about it, I should have realized that there was something odd in the way we were all laughing and joking. At the time, though, it seemed natural enough.

Even the commander unbent more than I'd ever known him to before—not that he was ever really very formidable, once you'd got used to him. But he never talked about himself, and back at the Inner Station no one would have dreamed of asking him to tell the story of his part in the first expedition to Mercury. And if they had, he certainly wouldn't have done so—yet he did now. He grumbled for a while, but not very effectively. Then he began to talk.

"Where shall I start?" he mused. "Well, there's not much to say about the voyage itself—it was just like any other trip. No one else had ever been so near the sun before, but the mirror-plating of our ship worked perfectly

and stopped us getting too hot by bouncing eighty per-
cent of the sun's rays straight off again.

"Our instructions were not to attempt a landing unless
we were quite sure it would be safe. So we got into an
orbit a thousand miles up and began to do a careful survey.

"You know, of course, that Mercury always keeps one
face turned toward the sun, so that it hasn't days or
nights as we have on earth. One side is in perpetual
darkness, the other in blazing light. However, there's a
narrow 'twilight' zone between the two hemispheres, where
the temperature isn't too extreme. We planned to come
down somewhere in this region, if we could find a good
landing place.

"We had our first surprise when we looked at the day
side of the planet. Somehow, everyone had always imagined that it would be very much like the moon—covered
with jagged craters and mountain ranges. But it wasn't.
There are no mountains at all on the part of Mercury
directly facing the sun, only a few low hills and great,
cracked plains. When we thought about it, the reason was
obvious. The temperature down there in that perpetual sunlight is over seven hundred degrees Fahrenheit. That's
much too low to melt rock, but it can soften it, and
gravity had done the rest. Over millions of years, any
mountains that might have existed on the day side of
Mercury had slowly collapsed, just as a block of pitch
flows on a hot day. Only round the rim of the night land,
where the temperature was far lower, were there any real
mountains.

"Our second surprise was to discover that there were
lakes down in that blazing inferno. Of course, they weren't
lakes of water, but of molten metal. Since no one has
been able to reach them yet, we don't know what metals
they are—probably lead and tin, with other things mixed
up with them. Lakes of solder, in fact! They may be pretty
valuable one day, if we can discover how to tap them."

The commander nodded his head thoughtfully, before
continuing.

"As you'll guess from this, we weren't anxious to land anywhere in the middle of the day side. So when we'd completed a photographic map we had a look at the night land.

"The only way we could do that was to illuminate it with flares. We went as close as we dared, less than a hundred miles up, and shot off billion candle power markers one after another, taking photographs as we did so. The flares, of course, shared our speed and traveled along with us until they burned out.

"It was a strange experience, knowing that we were shedding light on a land that had never seen the sun— a land where the only light for maybe millions of years had been that of the stars. If there was any life down there—which seemed about as unlikely as anything could be—it must be having quite a surprise! At least, that was my first thought as I watched our flares blasting that hidden land with their brilliance. Then I decided that any creatures of the night land would probably be completely blind, like the fish of our own ocean depths. Still, all this was fantasy. *Nothing* could possibly live down there in that perpetual darkness, at a temperature of almost four hundred degrees below freezing point. We know better, now, of course." He smiled.

"It was nearly a week before we risked a landing, and by that time we'd mapped the surface of the planet pretty thoroughly. The night land, and much of the twilight zone, is fairly mountainous, but there were plenty of flat regions that looked promising. We finally chose a large, shallow bowl on the edge of the day side.

"There's a trace of atmosphere on Mercury, but not enough for wings or parachutes to be of any use. So we had to land by rocket braking, just as you do on the moon. However often you do it, a rocket touchdown is always a bit unnerving, especially on a new world where you can't be perfectly sure that what *looks* like rock is anything of the sort.

"Well, it *was* rock, not one of those treacherous dust-drifts they have on the moon. The landing gear took up the impact so thoroughly that we hardly noticed it in the cabin. Then the motors cut out automatically and we were down, the first men to land on Mercury. The first living creatures, probably, ever to touch the planet.

"I said that we'd come down at the frontiers of the day side. That meant that the sun was a great, blinding disk right on the horizon. It was strange, seeing it almost fixed there, never rising or setting though, because Mercury has a very eccentric orbit, the sun does wobble to and fro through a considerable arc in the sky. Still, it never dropped *below* the horizon, and I always had the feeling that it was late afternoon and that night would fall shortly. It was hard to realize that 'night' and 'day' didn't mean anything here. . . .

"Exploring a new world sounds exciting, and so it is, I suppose. But it's also hard work—and dangerous, especially on a planet like Mercury. Our first job was to see that the ship couldn't get overheated, and we'd brought along some protective awnings for this purpose. Our 'sunshades,' we called them. They looked peculiar, but they did the job properly. We even had portable ones, like flimsy tents, to protect us if we stayed out in the open for any length of time. They were made of white nylon and reflected most of the sunlight, though they let through enough to provide all the warmth and light we wanted.

"We spent several weeks reconnoitering the day side, traveling up to twenty miles from the ship. That may not sound very far, but it's quite a distance when you've got to wear a space suit and carry all your supplies. We collected hundreds of mineral specimens and took thousands of readings with our instruments, sending back all the results we could by tight-beam radio to earth. It was impossible to go far enough into the day side to reach the lakes we'd seen. The nearest was over eight hundred miles away, and we couldn't afford the rocket fuel to go hopping around the planet. In any case, it would have been far too dangerous to go into that blazing furnace with our present, untried equipment."

The commander paused, staring thoughtfully into space

as if he could see beyond our cramped little cabin to the burning deserts of that distant world.

"Yes," he continued at last, "Mercury's *quite* a challenge. We can deal with cold easily enough, but heat's another problem. I suppose I shouldn't say that, because it was the cold that got me, not the heat. . . .

"The one thing we never expected to find on Mercury was life, though the moon should have taught us a lesson. No one had expected to find it there, either. And if anyone had said to me, 'Assuming that there *is* life on Mercury, where would you hope to find it?' I'd have replied, "Why, in the twilight zone, of course.' I'd have been wrong again.

"Though no one was very keen on the idea, we decided we ought to have at least one good look at the night land. We had to move the ship about a hundred miles to get clear of the twilight zone, and we landed on a low, flat hill a few miles from an interesting-looking range of mountains. We spent an anxious twenty-four hours before we were sure that it was safe to stay. The rock on which the ship was standing had a temperature of minus three hundred and fifty degrees, but our heaters could handle the situation. Even without them on, the temperature in the ship dropped very slowly, because there was a near vacuum around us and our silvered walls reflected back most of the heat we'd lose by radiation. We were living, in fact, inside a large thermos flask, and our bodies were also generating quite a bit of heat.

"Still, we couldn't learn much merely by sitting inside the ship; we had to put on our space suits and go out into the open. The suits we were using had been tested pretty thoroughly on the moon during the lunar night, which is almost as cold as it is on Mercury. But no test is ever quite like the real thing. That was why three of us went out. If one man got into trouble, the other two could get him back to the ship—we hoped.

"I was in that first party. We walked slowly round for about thirty minutes, taking things easily and reporting to the ship by radio. It wasn't as dark as we'd expected, thanks to Venus. She was hanging up there against the stars, incredibly brilliant and casting easily visible shadows. Indeed, she was too bright to look at directly for more than a few seconds, and then, using a filter to cut down the glare, one could easily see the tiny disk of the planet.

"The earth and moon were also visible, forming a beautiful double star just above the horizon. They also gave quite a lot of light, so we were never in complete darkness. But neither Venus nor earth gave the slightest heat to this frozen land.

"We couldn't lose the ship, because it was the most prominent object for miles around and we'd also fixed a powerful beacon on its nose. With some difficulty we broke off a few small specimens of rock and carried them back with us. As soon as we took them into the air lock, an extraordinary thing happened. They became instantly covered with frost, and drops of liquid began to form on them, dripping off to the floor and evaporating again. It was the air in the ship condensing on the bitterly cold fragments of stone. We had to wait half an hour before they had become sufficiently warm to handle.

"Once we were sure that our suits could withstand the conditions in the night land, we made longer trips, though we were never away from the ship for more than a couple of hours. We hadn't reached the mountains yet—they were just out of range. I used to spend a good deal of time examining them through the electronic telescope in the ship. There was enough light to make this possible.

"Then, one day, I saw something moving. I was so astonished that for a moment I sat frozen at the telescope, gaping foolishly through the eyepiece. Then I regained enough presence of mind to switch on the camera.

"You must have seen the film. It's not very good, of course, because the light was so weak. But it shows the mountain wall with a sort of landslide in the foreground and something large and white scrabbling round the rocks. When I saw it first it looked like a ghost and I don't mind saying that it scared me. Then the thrill of discovery banished every other feeling, and I concentrated on observing as much as I could.

"It wasn't a great deal, but I got the general impression of a roughly spherical body with at least four legs. Then it vanished, and it never reappeared.

"Of course, we dropped everything else and had a council of war. It was lucky for me that I'd taken the film, as otherwise everyone would have accused me of dreaming. We all agreed that we must try and get near the creature: the only question was whether it was dangerous.

"We had no weapons of any kind, but the ship carried a flare pistol which was intended for signaling. If it did nothing else, this should frighten any beast that attacked us. I carried the pistol, and my two companions—Borrell, the navigator, and Glynne, the radio operator, had a couple of stout bars. We also carried cameras and lighting equipment in the hope of getting some really good pictures. We felt that three was about the right number for the expedition. Fewer might not be safe and—well, if the thing was really dangerous, sending the whole crew would only make matters worse.

"It was five miles to the mountains, and it took us about an hour to reach them. The ship checked our course over the radio and we had an observer at the telescope, keeping a search in the neighborhood so that we'd have some warning if the creature turned up. I don't think we felt in any danger; we were all much too excited for that. And it was difficult to see what harm any animal could do to us inside the armor of our space suits as long as the helmets didn't get cracked. The low gravity and the extra strength that it gave us added to our confidence.

"At last we reached the rock slide and made a peculiar discovery. Something had been collecting stones and smashing them up; there were piles of broken fragments lying around. It was difficult to see what this meant, unless the creature we were seeking actually found its food among the rocks.

"I collected a few samples for analysis while Glynne

photographed our discovery and reported to the ship. Then we started to hunt around, keeping quite close together in case of trouble. The rock slide was about a mile across, and it seemed that the whole face of the mountain had crumbled and slid downward. We wondered what could have caused this, in the absence of any weather. Since there was no erosion, we couldn't guess how long ago the slip had occurred. It might have been a million years old—or a billion.

"Imagine us, then, scrambling across that jumble of broken rocks, with Earth and Venus hanging overhead like brilliant beacons and the lights of our ship burning reassuringly down on the horizon. By now I had practically decided that our quarry must be some kind of rock-eater, if only because there seemed no other kind of food on this desolate planet. I wished I knew enough about minerals to determine what substance this was.

"Then Glynne's excited shout rang in my earphones.

" 'There it is!' he yelled. 'By that cliff over there!'

"We just stood and stared, and I had my first good look at a Mercurian. It was more like a giant spider than anything else, or perhaps one of those crabs with long, spindly legs. Its body was a sphere about a yard across and was a silvery white. At first we thought it had four legs, but later we discovered that there were actually eight, a reserve set being carried tucked up close to the body. They were brought into action when the incredible cold of the rocks began to creep too far up the thick layers of insulating horn which formed its feet or hoofs. When the Mercurian got cold feet, it switched to another pair!

"It also had two handling limbs, which at the moment were busily engaged in searching among the rocks. They ended in elaborate, horny claws or pincers which looked as if they could be dangerous in a fight. There was no real head, but only a tiny bulge on the top of the spherical body. Later we discovered that this housed two large eyes, for use in the dim starlight of the night land and two small ones for excursions into the more brilliantly illuminated twilight zone—the sensitive large eyes then being kept tightly shut.

"We watched, fascinated, while the ungainly creature scuttled among the rocks, pausing now and again to seize a specimen and smash it to powder with those efficient-looking claws. Then something that might have been a tongue would flash out, too swiftly for the eye to follow, and the powder would be gobbled up.

" 'What do you think it's after?' asked Borrell. 'That rock seems pretty soft. I wonder if it's some kind of chalk?'

" 'Hardly,' I replied. 'It's the wrong color and chalk's only formed at the bottom of seas, anyway. There's never been free water on Mercury.'

" 'Shall we see how close we can get?' said Glynne. 'I can't take a good photo from here. It's an ugly-looking beast, but I don't think it can do us any harm. It'll probably run a mile as soon as it sees us.'

"I gripped the flare pistol more firmly and said, 'O.K. —let's go. But move slowly, and stop as soon as it spots us.'

"We were within a hundred feet before the creature showed any signs of interest in us. Then it pivoted on its stalklike legs and I could see its great eyes looking at us in the faint moonglow of Venus. Glynne said, 'Shall I use the flash? I can't take a good picture in this light.'

"I hesitated, then told him to go ahead. The creature gave a start as the brief explosion of light splashed over the landscape, and I heard Glynne's sigh of relief. 'That's *one* picture in the bag, anyway! Wonder if I can get a close-up?'

" 'No,' I ordered. 'That would certainly scare it or annoy it, which might be worse. I don't like the look of those claws. Let's try and prove that we're friends. You stay here and I'll go forward. Then it won't think we're ganging up on it.'

"Well, I still think the idea was good, but I didn't know much about the habits of Mercurians in those days. As I walked slowly forward the creature seemed to stiffen, like a dog over a bone—and for the same reason, I guessed. It stretched itself up to its full height, which was nearly eight feet, and then began to sway back and forth slightly, looking very much like a captive balloon in a breeze.

" 'Come back!' advised Borrell. 'It's annoyed. Better not take any chances.'

" 'I don't intend to,' I replied. 'It's not easy to walk backward in a space suit, but I'm going to try it now.'

"I'd retreated a few yards when, without moving from its position, the creature suddenly whipped out one of its arms and grabbed a stone. The motion was so human that I knew what was coming and instinctively covered my visor with my arm. A moment later something struck the lower part of my suit with a terrific crash. It didn't hurt me, but the whole carapace vibrated for a moment like a gong. For an anxious few seconds I held my breath, waiting for the fatal hiss of air. But the suit held, though I could see a deep dent on the left thigh. The next time I might not be so lucky, so I decided to use my 'weapon' as a distraction.

"The brilliant white flare floated slowly up toward the stars, flooding the landscape with harsh light and putting distant Venus to shame. And then something happened that we weren't to understand until much later. I'd noticed a pair of bulges on either side of the Mercurian's body, and as we watched they opened up like the wing cases of a beetle. Two wide, black wings unfurled— *wings*, on this almost airless world! I was so astonished that for a moment I was too surprised to continue my retreat. Then the flare slowly burned itself out, and as it guttered to extinction the velvet wings folded themselves and were tucked back into their cases.

"The creature made no attempt to follow, and we met no others on this occasion. As you can guess, we were sorely puzzled, and our colleagues back in the ship could hardly credit their ears when we told them what had happened. Now that we know the answer, of course, it seems simple enough. It always does.

"Those weren't really wings that we'd watched unfold,

though ages ago, when Mercury had an atmosphere, they had been. The creature I'd discovered was one of the most marvelous examples of adaptation known in the solar system. Its normal home is the twilight zone, but because the minerals it feeds on have been exhausted there it has to go foraging far into the night land. Its whole body has evolved to resist that incredible cold. That is the reason why it's silvery white, because this color radiates the least amount of heat. Even so, it can't stay in the night land indefinitely, but has to return to the twilight zone at intervals, just as on our own world a whale has to come up for air. When it sees the sun again, it spreads those black wings, which are really heat absorbers. I suppose my flare must have triggered off this reaction—or maybe even the small amount of heat given off by it was worth grabbing.

"The search for food must be desperate for nature to have taken such drastic steps. The Mercurians aren't really vicious beasts, but they have to fight among themselves for survival. Since the hard casing of the body is almost invulnerable, they go for the legs. A crippled night-lander is doomed, because he can't reach the twilight zone again before his stores of heat are exhausted. So they've learned to throw stones at each other's legs with great accuracy. My space suit must have puzzled the specimen I met, but it did its best to cripple me. As I soon discovered, it succeeded too well.

"We still don't know much about these creatures, despite the efforts that have been made to study them. And I've got a theory I'd like to see investigated. It seems to me that, just as some of the Mercurians have evolved so that they can forage into the cold of the night land, there may be another variety that's gone into the burning day land. I wonder what *they'll* be like?"

The commander stopped talking. I got the impression that he didn't really want to continue. But our waiting silence was too much for him, and he carried on.

"We were walking back slowly to the ship, still arguing about the creature we'd met, when suddenly I realized that something had gone wrong. My feet were getting cold, very cold. The heat was ebbing out of my space suit, sucked away by the frozen rocks beneath me.

"I knew at once what had happened. The blow my suit had received had broken the leg heater-circuits. There was nothing that could be done until I got back to the ship and I had four miles still ahead of me.

"I told the others what had happened and we put on all the speed we could. Every time my feet touched the ground I could feel that appalling chill striking deeper. After a while all sensation was lost; that at least was something to be thankful for. My legs were just wooden stumps with no feeling at all, and I was still two miles from the ship when I couldn't move them any more. The joints of the suit were freezing cold.

"After that my companions had to carry me, and I must have lost consciousness for a while. I revived once while we were still some way from the end of that journey, and for a moment I thought I must be delirious. For the land all around me was ablaze with light. Brilliant colored streamers flickered across the sky and overhead, waves of crimson fire marched beneath the stars. In my dazed state, it was some time before I realized what had happened. The Aurora, which is far more brilliant on Mercury than on the earth, had suddenly decided to switch on one of its displays. It was ironic, though at the time I could scarcely appreciate it. For, although the land all around me seemed to be burning, I was swiftly freezing to death.

"Well, we made it somehow, though I don't remember ever entering the ship. When I came back to consciousness, we were on the way back to earth. But my legs were still on Mercury."

No one said anything for a long time. Then the pilot glanced at his chronometer and exclaimed, "Wow! I should have made my course check ten minutes ago!" That broke the suspense, and our imaginations came rushing back from Mercury.

For the next few minutes the pilot was busy with the

ship's position-finding gear. The first space navigators had only the stars to guide them, but now there were all sorts of radio and radar aids. One only bothered about the rather tedious astronomical methods when a long way from home, out of range of the earth stations.

I was watching the pilot's fingers flying across the calculator keyboard, envying his effortless skill, when suddenly he froze over his desk. Then, very carefully, he pecked at the keys and set up his calculations again. An answer came up on the register, and I knew that something was wrong! For a moment the pilot stared at his figures as if unable to believe them. Then he loosened himself from the straps holding him to his seat and swiftly moved over to the nearest observation port.

I was the only one who noticed. The others were now quietly reading in their bunks or trying to snatch some sleep. There was a port only a few feet away from me and I headed for it. Out there in space was the earth, nearly full—the planet toward which we were slowly falling.

Then an icy band seemed to grip my chest and for a moment I completely stopped breathing. By this time, I knew, earth should already be appreciably larger as we dropped in from the orbit of the hospital. Yet unless my eyes deceived me, it was *smaller* than when I had last seen it. I looked again at the pilot, and his face confirmed my fears.

We were heading out into space.

9 THE SHOT FROM THE MOON

✦✦✦✦✦✦✦✦✦✦✦✦✦✦✦✦✦✦✦✦✦✦✦✦✦✦✦✦✦✦✦✦✦✦✦

"COMMANDER DOYLE," said the pilot, in a very small voice. "Will you come here a minute?" The commander stirred in his bunk.

"Confound it, I was nearly asleep!"

"I'm sorry, but—well, there's been an accident. We're—we're in an escape orbit."

"What!"

The roar woke up everyone else. With a mighty heave, the commander left his bunk and headed for the control desk. There was a rapid conference with the unhappy pilot; then the commander ordered: "Get me the nearest Relay Station. I'm taking over."

"What happened?" I whispered to Tim Benton.

"I think I know," said Tim, "but wait a minute before we jump to conclusions."

It was almost a quarter of an hour before anyone bothered to explain things to me, a quarter of an hour of furious activity, radio calls, and lightning calculations. Then Norman Powell, who like me had nothing to do but watch, took pity on my ignorance.

"This ship's got a curse on it," he said in disgust. "The pilot has made the one navigation error you'd think was impossible. He should have cut our speed by point nine miles a second. Instead, he applied power in exactly the wrong direction and we've *gained* speed by that amount. So instead of falling earthward, we're heading out into space."

Even to me, it seemed hard to imagine that anyone could make such an extraordinary mistake. Later, I discovered that it was one of those things, like landing an aircraft with wheels up, that it isn't as difficult to do as it sounds. Aboard a spaceship in free orbit, there's no way of telling in which direction and at what speed you're moving. Everything has to be done by instruments and calculations, and if at a certain stage a minus sign is taken for a plus, then it's easy to point the ship in exactly the wrong direction before applying power.

Of course, one is supposed to make other checks to prevent such mistakes. Somehow they hadn't worked this time or the pilot hadn't applied them. It wasn't until a long time later that we found the full reason. The jammed oxygen valve, not the unhappy pilot, was the real culprit. I'd been the only one who had actually fainted, but the others had all been suffering from oxygen starvation. It's a very dangerous complaint, because you don't realize that there's anything wrong with you. Indeed, you can be making all sorts of stupid mistakes, yet feel that you're right on top of your job.

But it was not much use finding out why the accident had happened. The problem now was—what should be done next?

The extra speed we'd been given was just enough to put us into an escape orbit. In other words, we were traveling so fast that the earth could never pull us back. We were heading out into space, somewhere beyond the orbit of the moon, and wouldn't know our exact path until we got HAVOC to work it out for us. Commander Doyle had radioed our position and velocity, and now we had to wait for further instructions.

The situation was serious, but not hopeless. We still had a considerable amount of fuel—the reserve intended for the approach to the Inner Station. If we used it now, we could at least prevent ourselves flying away from earth, but we should then be traveling in a new orbit that might not take us anywhere near one of the space stations. Whatever happened, we had to get fresh fuel from somewhere, and as quickly as possible. The short-range ship in which we were traveling wasn't designed for long excursions into space and carried only a limited oxygen supply. We had enough for about a hundred hours. If help couldn't reach us by that time, it would be just too bad.

It's a funny thing, but though I was now in real danger for the first time, I didn't feel half as frightened as I did when we were caught by Cuthbert or when the "meteor" holed the classroom. Somehow, this seemed different. We had several days' breathing space before the crisis would be upon us. And we all had such confidence in Commander Doyle that we were sure he could get us out of this mess.

Though we couldn't really appreciate it at the time, there was certainly something ironic about the fact that we'd have been quite safe if we'd stuck to the *Morning Star* and not ultra-cautiously decided to go home on another ship.

We had to wait for nearly fifteen minutes before the computing staff on the Inner Station worked out our new orbit and radioed it back to us. Commander Doyle plotted our path, and we all craned over his shoulder to see what course our ship was going to follow.

"We're heading for the moon," he said, tracing out the dotted line with his finger. "We'll pass its orbit in about forty hours, near enough for its gravitational field to have quite an effect. If we want to use some rocket braking, we can let it capture us."

"Wouldn't that be a good idea? At least it would stop us heading out into space."

The commander rubbed his chin thoughtfully.

"I don't know," he said. "It depends on whether there are any ships on the moon that can come up to us."

"Can't we land on the moon ourselves, near one of the settlements?" asked Norman.

"No. We've not enough fuel for the descent. The motors aren't powerful enough, anyway—you ought to know that."

Norman subsided, and the cabin was filled with a long, thoughtful silence that began to get on my nerves. I wished I could help with some bright ideas, but it wasn't likely they'd be any better than Norman's.

"The trouble is," said the commander at last, "that there are so many factors involved. There are several *possible* solutions to our problems. What we want to find is the *most economical* one. It's going to cost a fortune if we have to call a ship up from the moon, just to match our speed and transfer a few tons of fuel. That's the obvious, brute-force answer."

It was a relief to know that there *was* an answer. That was really all that I wanted to hear. Someone else would have to worry about the bill.

Suddenly the pilot's face lit up. He had been sunk in gloom until now and hadn't contributed a word to the conversation.

"I've got it!" he said. "We should have thought of it before! What's wrong with using the launcher down in Hipparchus? That should be able to shoot us up some fuel without any trouble, as far as one can tell from this chart."

The conversation then grew very animated and technical, and I was rapidly left behind. Ten minutes later the general gloom in the cabin began to disperse, so I guessed that some satisfactory conclusion had been reached. When the discussion had died away, and all the radio calls had been made, I got Tim into a corner and threatened to keep bothering him until he explained what was going on.

"Surely, Roy," he said, "you know about the Hipparchus launcher?"

"Isn't it that magnetic thing that shoots fuel tanks up to rockets orbiting the moon?"

"Of course. It's an electro-magnetic track about five miles long, running east and west across the crater Hipparchus. They chose that spot because it's near the center of the moon's disk and the fuel refineries aren't far away. Ships waiting to be refueled get into an orbit round the moon, and at the right time they shoot up the containers into the same orbit. The ship's got to do a bit of maneuvering by rocket power to 'home' on the tank, but it's much cheaper than doing the whole job by rockets."

"What happens to the empty tanks?"

"That depends on the launching speed. Sometimes they crash back on the moon; after all, there's plenty of room for them to come down without doing any harm! But usually they're given lunar escape velocity, so they just get lost in space. There's even more out *there!*"

"I see. We're going near enough to the moon for a fuel tank to be shot out to us."

"Yes; they're doing the calculations now. Our orbit will pass behind the moon, about five thousand miles above the surface. They'll match our speed as accurately as they can with the launcher, and we'll have to do the rest under our own power. It'll mean using some of our fuel, of course, but the investment will be worth it!"

"And when will all this happen?"

"In about forty hours. We're waiting for the exact figures now."

I was probably the only one who felt really pleased with the prospect, now that I knew we were reasonably safe. To the others, this was a tedious waste of time, but it was going to give me an opportunity of seeing the moon at close quarters. This was certainly far more than I could have dared hope when I left earth. The Inner Station already seemed a long way behind me.

Hour by hour earth dwindled and the moon grew larger in the sky ahead. There was very little to do, apart from routine checks of the instruments and regular radio calls to the various space stations and the lunar base. Most of the time was spent sleeping and playing cards, but once I was given a chance to speak to Mom and Pop, way back on earth. They sounded a bit worried, and for the first time I realized that we were probably making headlines. However, I think I made it clear that I was enjoying myself and there was no real need for any alarm.

All the necessary arrangements had been agreed upon, and there was nothing to do but wait until we swept past the moon and made our appointment with the fuel container. Though I had often watched the moon through telescopes, both from earth and from the Inner Station, it was a very different matter to see the great plains and mountains with my own unaided eyes. We were now so close that all the larger craters were easily visible along the band dividing night from day. The line of sunrise had just passed the center of the disk, and it was early dawn down there in Hipparchus, where they were preparing for our rescue. I asked permission to borrow the ship's telescope and peered down into the great crater.

It seemed that I was hanging in space only fifty miles above the moon. Hipparchus completely filled the field of vision; it was impossible to take it all in at once glance. The sunlight was slanting over the ruined walls of the crater, casting mile-long pools of inky shadow. Here and there upthrust peaks caught the first light of dawn and blazed like beacons in the darkness all around them.

There were other lights in the crater shadows, lights arranged in tiny, geometric patterns. I was looking down on one of the lunar settlements. Now hidden from me in the darkness were the great chemical plants, the pressurized domes, the spaceports and the power stations that drove the launching track. In a few hours they would be clearly visible as the sun rose above the mountains, but by then we should have passed behind the moon and the earthward side would be hidden from us.

And then I saw it, a thin bar of light stretching in a dead straight line across the darkened plain. I was looking at the floodlights of the launching track, ranged like the lamps along an arterial road. By their illumination, space-suited engineers would be checking the great electromagnets and seeing that the cradle ran freely in its guides. The fuel tank would be waiting at the head of the track, already loaded and ready to be placed on the cradle when the time arrived. If it had been daylight down there, perhaps I could have seen the actual launch. There would have been a tiny speck racing along the track, moving more and more swiftly as the generators poured their power into the magnets. It would leave the end of the launcher at a speed of over five thousand miles an hour, too fast for the moon ever to pull it back. As it traveled almost horizontally, the surface of the moon would curve away beneath it and it would sweep out into space to meet us, if all went well, three hours later.

I think the most impressive moment of all my adventures came when the ship passed behind the moon, and I saw with my own eyes the land that had remained hidden from human sight until the coming of the rocket. It was true that I had seen many films and photographs of the moon's other side, and it was also true that it was very much the same as the visible face. Yet somehow the thrill remained. I thought of all the astronomers who had spent their lives charting the moon, but had never seen the land over which I was now passing. What would they have given for the opportunity that had now come to me, and come quite by chance, without any real effort on my part!

I had almost forgotten earth when Tim Benton drew my attention to it again. It was sinking swiftly toward the lunar horizon: the moon was rising up to eclipse it as we swept along in our great arc. A blinding blue-green crescent, the South Polar cap almost too brilliant to look upon, the reflection of the sun forming a pool of fire in the Pacific Ocean—that was my home, now a quarter of million miles away. I watched it drop behind the cruel lunar peaks until only the faint, misty rim was visible; then even this disappeared. The sun was still with us, but the earth had gone. Until this moment it had always been with us in the sky, part of the background of things. Now I had only sun, moon and stars.

The fuel container was already on its way up to meet us. It had been launched an hour before, and we had been told by radio that it was proceeding on the correct orbit. The moon's gravitational field would curve its path and we would pass within a few hundred miles of it. Our job then was to match speeds by careful use of our remaining fuel and, when we had coupled our ship up to the tank, pump across its contents. Then we could turn for home and the empty container would coast on out into space to join the rest of the debris circulating in the solar system.

"But just suppose," I said anxiously to Norman Powell, "that they score a direct hit on us! After all, the whole thing's rather like shooting a gun at a target. And *we're* the target."

Norman laughed.

"It'll be moving very slowly when it comes up to us, and we'll spot it in our radar when it's a long way off. So there's no danger of a collision. By the time it is really close, we'll have matched speeds and if we bump it'll be about as violent as two snowflakes meeting head on."

That was reassuring, though I still didn't really like the idea of this projectile from the moon tearing up at us through space. . . .

We picked up the signals from the fuel container when it was still a thousand miles away, not with our radar, but thanks to the tiny radio beacon that all these missiles carried to aid their detection. After this I kept out of the way while Commander Doyle and the pilot made our rendezvous in space. It was a delicate operation, this jockeying of a ship until it matched the course of the still-invisible projectile. Our fuel reserves were too slim to permit any more mistakes, and everyone breathed a great sigh of relief when the stubby, shining cylinder was hanging beside us.

The transfer took only about ten minutes, and when our pumps had finished their work the earth had emerged from behind the moon's shield. It seemed a good omen. We were once more masters of the situation and in sight of home again.

I was watching the radar screen, because no one else wanted to use it, when we turned on the motors again. The empty fuel container, which had now been uncoupled, seemed to fall slowly astern. Actually, of course, it was *we* who were falling back, checking our speed to return earthward. The fuel capsule would go shooting on out into space, thrown away, now that its task was completed.

The extreme range of our radar was about five hundred miles, and I watched the bright spot representing the fuel container drift slowly toward the edge of the screen. It was the only object near enough to produce an echo. The volume of space which our beams were sweeping probably contained quite a number of meteors, but they were far too small to produce a visible signal. Yet there was something fascinating about watching even this almost empty screen—empty, that is, apart from an occasional sparkle of light caused by electrical interference. It made me visualize the thousand-mile-diameter globe at whose center we were traveling. Nothing of any size could enter that globe without our invisible radio fingers detecting it and giving the alarm.

We were now safely back on course, no longer racing out into space. Commander Doyle had decided not to return directly to the Inner Station, because our oxygen reserve was getting low. Instead, we would home on one of the three Relay Stations, twenty-two thousand miles above the earth. The ship could be reprovisioned there before we continued the last lap of our journey.

I was just about to switch off the radar screen when I saw a faint spark of light at extreme range. It vanished a second later as our beam moved into another sector of space, and I waited until it had swept through the complete cycle, wondering if I'd been mistaken. Were there any other spaceships around here? It was quite possible, of course.

There was no doubt about it. The spark appeared again,

in the same position. I knew how to work the scanner controls and stopped the beam sweeping so that it locked on to the distant echo. It was just under five hundred miles away, moving very slowly with respect to us. I looked at it thoughtfully for a few seconds and then called Tim. It was probably not important enough to bother the commander. However, there was just the chance that it was a really large meteor, and they were always worth investigating. One that gave an echo this size would be much too big to bring home, but we might be able to chip bits off it for souvenirs—if we matched speed with it, of course.

Tim started the scanner going as soon as I handed over the controls. He thought I'd picked up our discarded fuel container again, which annoyed me since it showed little faith in my common sense. But he soon saw that it was in a different part of the sky and his skepticism vanished.

"It must be a spaceship," he said, "though it doesn't seem a large enough echo for that. We'll soon find out. If it's a ship, it'll be carrying a radio beacon."

He tuned our receiver to the beacon frequency, but without results. There were a few ships at great distances in other parts of the sky, but nothing as close as this.

Norman had now joined us and was looking over Tim's shoulder.

"If it's a meteor," he said, "let's hope it's a nice lump of platinum or something equally valuable. Then we can retire for life."

"Hey!" I exclaimed. "*I* found it!"

"I don't think that counts. You're not on the crew and shouldn't be here anyway."

"Don't worry," said Tim, "no one's ever found anything except iron in meteors, at least not in any quantity. The most you can expect to run across out here is a chunk of nickel steel, probably so tough that you won't even be able to saw off a piece as a souvenir."

By now we had worked out the course of the object and discovered that it would pass within twenty miles of us. If we wished to make contact, we'd have to change our velocity by about two hundred miles an hour—not much, but it would waste some of our hard-won fuel and the commander certainly wouldn't allow it, if it was merely a question of satisfying our curiosity.

"How big would it have to be to produce an echo this bright?" I asked.

"You can't tell," said Tim. "It depends on what it's made of and which way it's pointing. A spaceship *could* produce a signal as small as that, if we were only seeing it end on."

"I think I've found it," said Norman suddenly. "And it *isn't* a meteor. You have a look."

He had been searching with the ship's telescope, and I took his place at the eyepiece, getting there just ahead of Tim. Against a background of faint stars a roughly cylindrical object, brilliantly lit by the sunlight, was very slowly revolving in space. Even at first glance I could see it was artificial. When I had watched it turn through a complete revolution, I could see that it was streamlined and had a pointed nose. It looked much more like an old-time artillery shell than a modern rocket. The fact that it was streamlined meant that it couldn't be an empty fuel container from the launcher in Hipparchus; the tanks it shot up were plain, stubby cylinders, since streamlining was no use on the airless moon.

Commander Doyle stared through the telescope for a long time after we called him over. Finally, to my joy, he remarked: "Whatever it is, we'd better have a look at it and make a report. We can spare the fuel, and it will only take a few minutes."

Our ship spun round in space as we began to make the course correction. The rockets fired for a few seconds, our new path was rechecked, and the rockets operated again. After several shorter bursts, we had come to within a mile of the mysterious object and began to edge toward it under the gentle impulse of the steering jets alone. Through all these maneuvers it was impossible to use the telescope, so when I next saw my discovery it was only a hundred yards beyond our port, very gently approaching us.

It was artificial, all right, and a rocket of some kind. What it was doing out here near the moon we could only guess, and several theories were put forward. Since it was only about ten feet long, it might be one of the automatic reconnaissance missiles sent out in the early days of spaceflight. Commander Doyle didn't think this likely, because as far as he knew, they'd all been accounted for. Besides, it seemed to have none of the radio and TV equipment such missiles would carry.

It was painted a very bright red, an odd color, I thought, for anything in space. There was some lettering on the side—apparently in English, though I couldn't make out the words at this distance. As the projectile slowly revolved, a black pattern on a white background came into view, but went out of sight before I could interpret it. I waited until it came into view again. By this time the little rocket had drifted considerably closer and was now only fifty feet away.

"I don't like the looks of that thing," Tim Benton said, half to himself. "That color, for instance, red's the sign of danger."

"Don't be an old woman," scoffed Norman. "If it was a bomb or something like that, it certainly wouldn't advertise the fact."

Then the pattern I'd glimpsed before swam back into view. Even on the first sight, there had been something uncomfortably familiar about it. Now there was no longer any doubt.

Clearly painted on the side of the slowly approaching missile was the symbol of death—the skull and crossbones.

◆◆◆◆◆◆◆◆◆◆◆◆◆◆◆◆◆◆◆◆◆◆◆◆◆◆◆◆◆◆◆◆◆◆◆◆◆

COMMANDER DOYLE MUST HAVE seen that ominous warning as quickly as we did, for an instant later our rockets thundered briefly. The crimson missile veered slowly aside and started to recede once more into space. At its moment of closest approach, I was able to read the words painted below the skull and crossbones—and I understood. The notice read:

WARNING!
RADIOACTIVE WASTE!
ATOMIC ENERGY COMMISSION

"I wish we had a Geiger counter on board," said the commander thoughtfully. "Still, by this time it can't be very dangerous and I don't expect we've had much of a dose. But we'll all have to have a blood count when we get back to base."

"How long do you think it's been up here, sir?" asked Norman.

"Let's think—I believe they started getting rid of dangerous waste this way back in the 1970's. They didn't do it for long; the space corporations soon put a stop to it! Nowadays, of course, we know to deal with all the by-products of the atomic piles, but back in the early days there were a lot of radio isotopes they couldn't handle. Rather a drastic way of getting rid of them, and a short-sighted solution too!"

"I've heard about these waste containers," said Tim, "but I thought they'd all been collected and the stuff in them buried somewhere on the moon."

"Not this one, apparently. But it soon will be when we report it. Good work, Malcolm! You've done your bit to make space safer!"

I was pleased at the compliment, though still a little worried lest we'd received a dangerous dose of radiation from the decaying isotopes in their celestial coffin. Luckily my fears turned out to be groundless, for we had left the neighborhood too quickly to come to any harm.

We also discovered, a good while later, the history of this stray missile. The Atomic Energy Commission is still a bit ashamed of this episode in its history, and it was some time before it gave the whole story. Finally it admitted the dispatch of a waste container in 1981 that had been intended to crash on the moon but had never done so. The astronomers had a lot of fun working out how the thing had got into the orbit where we found it. It was a complicated story involving the gravities of the earth, sun and moon.

Our detour had not lost us a great deal of time, and we were only a few minutes behind schedule when we came sweeping into the orbit of Relay Station Two, the one that sits above Latitude 30° East, over the middle of Africa. I was now used to seeing peculiar objects in space, so the first sight of the station didn't surprise me in the least. It consisted of a flat, rectangular lattice-work, with one side facing the earth. Covering this face were hundreds of small, concave reflectors, focusing systems that beamed the radio signals to the planet beneath, or collected them on the way up.

We approached cautiously, making contact with the back of the station. A pilot who let his ship pass in front of it was very unpopular, as he might cause a temporary failure on thousands of circuits, while blocking the radio beams. For the whole of the planet's long-distance services and most of the radio and TV networks were routed through the Relay Stations. As I looked more closely, I saw that there were two other sets of radio reflector systems, aimed not at earth but in the two directions sixty degrees away from it. These were handling the beams to the other two stations, so that altogether the three formed a vast triangle, slowly rotating with the turning earth.

We spent only twelve hours at the Relay Station, while our ship was overhauled and reprovisioned. I never saw the pilot again, though I heard later that he had been partly exonerated from blame. When we continued our interrupted journey, it was with a fresh captain, who showed no willingness to talk about his colleague's fate. Space pilots form a very select and exclusive club and never let each other down or discuss each other's mistakes, at least, not to people outside their trade union. I suppose you can hardly blame them, since theirs is one of the most responsible jobs that exists.

The living arrangements aboard the Relay Station were much the same as on the Inner Station, so I won't spend any time describing them. In any case, we weren't there long enough to see much of the place, and everyone was too busy to waste time showing us around. The TV people did ask us to make one appearance to describe our adventures since leaving the hospital. The interview took place in a makeshift studio, so tiny that it wouldn't hold us all, and we had to slip in quietly one by one when a signal was given. It seemed funny to find no better arrangements here at the very heart of the world's TV network. Still, it was reasonable enough because a "live" broadcast from the Relay Station was a very rare event indeed.

We also had a brief glimpse of the main switch room, though I'm afraid it didn't mean a great deal to us. There were acres of dials and colored lights, with men sitting here and there looking at screens and turning knobs. Soft voices, in every language, came through the loud-speakers. As we went from one operator to another we saw football games, string quartets, air races, ice hockey, art displays, puppet shows, grand opera—a cross section of the world's entertainment, all depending on these three tiny metal rafts, twenty-two thousand miles up in the sky. As I looked at *some* of the programs that were going out, I wondered if it was really worth it.

Not all the Relay Station's business was concerned with earth, by any means. The interplanetary circuits passed through here: if Mars wished to call Venus, it was some-times convenient to route messages through the earth re-lays. We listened to some of these messages, nearly all high-speed telegraphy, so they didn't mean anything to us. Because it takes several minutes for radio waves to bridge the gulf between even the nearest planets, you can't have conversation with someone on another world. (Except the moon—and even there you have to put up with an annoying time-lag of nearly three seconds before you can get any answer.) The only speech that was coming over the Martian circuit was a talk beamed to earth for rebroadcasting by a radio commentator. He was discus-sing local politics and the last season's crop. It all sounded rather dull.

Though I was there only a short time, one thing about the Relay Station did impress me very strongly. Everywhere else I'd been, one could look "down" at the earth and watch it turning on its axis, bringing new continents into view with the passing hours. But here there was no such change. The earth kept the same face turned forever to-ward the station. It was true that night and day passed across the planet beneath, but with every dawn and sun-set, the station was still in exactly the same place. It was poised eternally above a spot in Uganda, two hundred miles from Lake Victoria. Because of this, it was hard to believe that the station was moving at all, though actually it was traveling round the earth at over six thousand miles an hour. But because it took exactly one day to make the circuit, it would remain hanging over Africa forever —just as the other two stations hung above the opposite coasts of the Pacific.

This was only one of the ways in which the whole atmosphere aboard the Relay seemed quite different from that down on the Inner Station. The men here were doing a job that kept them in touch with everything happening on earth, often before earth knew it itself. Yet they were also on the frontiers of real space, for there was nothing else between them and the orbit of the moon. It was a strange situation, and I wished I could have stayed longer.

Unless there were any more accidents, my holiday in space was coming to an end. I'd already missed the ship that was supposed to take me home, but this didn't help me as much as I'd hoped. The plan now, I gathered, was to send me over to the Residential Station and put me aboard the regular ferry, so that I'd be going down to earth with the passengers homeward bound from Mars or Venus.

Our trip back to the Inner Station was uneventful and rather tedious. We couldn't persuade Commander Doyle to tell any more stories, and I think he was a bit ashamed of himself for being so talkative on the outward journey. This time, too, he was taking no chances with the pilot.

It seemed like coming home when the familiar chaos of the Inner Station swam into view. Nothing much had changed. Some ships had gone and others taken their place, that was all. The other apprentices were waiting for us in the air lock, an informal reception committee. They gave the commander a cheer as he came aboard, though afterward there was a lot of good-natured leg-pulling about our various adventures. In particular, the fact that the *Morning Star* was still out at the hospital caused numerous complaints, and we never succeeded in getting Commander Doyle to take all the blame for this.

I spent most of my last day aboard the station collecting autographs and souvenirs. The best memento of my stay was something quite unexpected—a beautiful little model of the station, made out of plastic and presented to me by the other boys. It pleased me so much that I was quite tongue-tied and didn't know how to thank them, but I guess they realized the way I felt.

At last everything was packed, and I could only hope my luggage was inside the weight limit. There was only one good-by left to make.

Commander Doyle was sitting at his desk, just as I'd seen him at our first meeting. But he wasn't so terrifying now, for I'd grown to know and admire him. I hoped that I'd not been too much of a nuisance and tried to say so. The commander grinned.

"It might have been worse," he said. "On the whole you kept out of the way pretty well, though you managed to get into some—ah—unexpected places. I'm wondering whether to send World Airways a bill for the extra fuel you used on our little voyage. It must come to a sizable amount."

I thought it best not to say anything, and presently he continued, after ruffling through the papers on his desk.

"I suppose you realize, Roy, that a goodly number of youngsters apply for jobs here and not many get them. The qualifications are too steep. Well, I've kept my eye on you in the last few weeks and have noticed how you've been shaping up. If when you're old enough—that will be in a couple of years, won't it?—you want to put your name down, I'll be glad to make a recommendation."

"Why, thank you, sir!"

"Of course, there will be a tremendous amount of study to be done. You've seen most of the fun and games, not the hard work. And you've not had to sit up here for months waiting for your leave to come along and wondering why you ever left earth."

There was nothing I could say to this; it was a problem

that must hit the commander harder than anyone else in the station.

He propelled himself out of his seat with his left hand, stretching out the right one toward me. As we shook hands, I again recalled our first meeting. How long ago that now seemed! And I suddenly realized that, though I'd seen him every day, I'd almost forgotten that Commander Doyle was legless. He was so perfectly adapted to his surroundings that the rest of us seemed freaks. It was an object lesson in what will-power and determination could do.

I had a surprise when I reached the air lock. Though I hadn't really given it any thought, I'd assumed that one of the normal ferry rockets was going to take me over to the Residential Station for my rendezvous with the ship for earth. Instead, there was the ramshackle *Skylark of Space,* her mooring lines drifting slackly. I wondered what our exclusive neighbors would think when this peculiar object arrived at their doorsteps, and guessed that it had probably been arranged especially to annoy them.

Tim Benton and Ronnie Jordan made up the crew and helped me get my luggage through the air lock. They looked doubtfully at the number of parcels I was carrying, and asked me if I knew what interplanetary freight charges were. Luckily, the homeward run is by far the cheapest, and though I had some awkward moments, I got everything through.

The great revolving drum of the Residential Station slowly expanded ahead of us: the untidy collection of domes and pressure-corridors that had been my home for so long dwindled astern. Very cautiously, Tim brought the *Skylark* up to the axis of the station. I couldn't see exactly what happened then, but big, jointed arms came out to meet us and drew us slowly in until the air locks clamped together.

"Well, so long," said Ron. "I guess we'll be seeing you again."

"I hope so," I said, wondering if I should mention

Commander Doyle's offer. "Come and see me when you're down on earth."

"Thanks, I'll do my best. Hope you have a good ride down."

I shook hands with them both, feeling pretty miserable as I did so. Then the doors folded back, and I went through into the flying hotel that had been my neighbor for so many days, but which I'd never visited before.

The air lock ended in a wide circular corridor, and waiting for me was a uniformed steward. That at once set the tone of the place: after having to do things for myself, I felt rather foolish as I handed over my luggage. And I wasn't used to being called "sir."

I watched with interest as the steward carefully placed my property against the wall of the corridor and told me to take my place beside it. Then there was a faint vibration, and I remembered the ride in the centrifuge I'd had back at the hospital. The same thing was happening here. The corridor was starting to rotate, matching the spin of the station, and centrifugal force was giving me weight again. Not until the two rates of spin were equal would I be able to go through into the rest of the station.

Presently a buzzer sounded, and I knew that our speeds had been matched. The force gluing me to the curved wall was very small, but it would increase as I got farther from the center of the station, until at the very rim it was equal to one earth gravity. I was in no hurry to experience that again, after my days of complete weightlessness.

The corridor ended in a doorway which led, much to my surprise, into an elevator cage. There was a short ride in which curious things seemed to happen to the vertical direction and then the door opened to reveal a large hall. I could hardly believe that I was not on earth. This might be the foyer of any luxury hotel. There was the reception desk with the residents making their inquiries and complaints, the uniformed staff was hurrying to and fro and from time to time someone was being paged over the speaker system. Only the long, graceful bounds

with which people walked revealed that this wasn't earth.
And above the reception desk was a large notice:

GRAVITY ON THIS FLOOR=⅓RD EARTH

That, I realized, would make it just about right for
the returning Martian colonists. Probably all the people
around me had come from the Red Planet, or were preparing to go there.

When I had checked in I was given a tiny room,
just large enough to hold a bed, a chair and a washbasin.
It was so strange to see freely flowing water again that the
first thing I did was to turn on the tap and watch a pool
of liquid form at the bottom of the basin. Then I suddenly realized that there must be baths here as well, so
with a whoop of joy I set off in search of one. I had
grown very tired of showers, and all the bother that went
with them.

So that was how I spent most of my first evening at
the Residential Station. All around me were travelers
who had come back from far worlds with stories of
strange adventures. But they could wait until tomorrow.
For the present I was going to enjoy one of the experiences that gravity *did* make possible, lying in a mass
of water which didn't try to turn itself into a giant,
drifting raindrop.

11 STARLIGHT HOTEL

◆◆◆

IT WAS LATE IN THE "evening" when I arrived aboard
the Residential Station. Time here had been geared to the
cycle of nights and days that existed down on earth. Every
twenty-four hours the lights dimmed, a hushed silence de-
scended, and the residents went to bed. Outside the walls
of the station the sun might be shining, or it might be in
eclipse behind the earth—it made no difference here in
this world of wide, curving corridors, thick carpets, soft
lights and quietly whispering voices. We had our own time
and no one took any notice of the sun.

I didn't sleep well my first night under gravity, even
though I had only a third of the weight to which I'd been
accustomed all my life. Breathing was difficult, and I had
unpleasant dreams. Again and again I seemed to be climbing a steep hill with a great load on my back. My legs
were aching, my lungs panting, and the hill stretched

endlessly ahead. However long I toiled, I never reached the top.

At last, however, I managed to doze off, and remembered nothing until a steward woke me with breakfast, which I ate from a little tray fixed over my bed. Though I was anxious to see the station, I took my time over this meal. This was a novel experience which I wanted to savor to the fullest. Breakfast in bed was rare enough, but to have it aboard a space station as well was really something!

When I had dressed, I started to explore my new surroundings. The first thing I had to get used to was the fact that the floors were all curved. (Of course, I also had to get used to the idea that there *were* floors anyway, after doing without up and down for so long.) The reason for this was simple enough. I was now living on the inside of a giant cylinder that slowly turned on its axis. Centrifugal force, the same force that held the station in the sky, was acting once again, gluing me to the side of the revolving drum. If you walked straight ahead, you could go right round the circumference of the station and come back to where you started. At any point, "up," would be toward the central axis of the cylinder, which meant that someone standing a few yards away, farther round the curve of the station, would appear to be tilted toward you. Yet to them, everything would be perfectly normal and *you* would be the one who was tilted! It was confusing at first, but like everything else, you got used to it after a while. The designers of the station had gone in for some clever tricks of decoration to hide what was happening, and in the smaller rooms the curve of the floor was too slight to be noticed.

The station wasn't merely a single cylinder, but three, one inside the other. As you moved out from the center, so the sense of weight increased. The innermost cylinder was the "One Third Earth Gravity" floor, and because it was nearest to the air locks on the station's axis it was devoted mainly to handling the passengers and their luggage. There was a saying that if you sat opposite the reception desk long enough, you'd see everyone of importance on the four planets.

Surrounding this central cylinder was the more spacious "Two Thirds Earth Gravity" floor. You passed from one floor to the other either by elevators or by curiously curved stairways. It was an odd experience, going down one of these stairs. At first I found it took quite a bit of will-power, for I was not yet accustomed even to a third of my earth weight. As I walked slowly down the steps, gripping the handrail very firmly, I seemed to grow steadily heavier. When I reached the floor, my movements were so slow and leaden that I imagined that everyone was looking at me. However, I soon grew used to the feeling, I had to, if I was ever going to return to earth!

Most of the passengers were on this "Two Thirds Gravity" floor. Most of them were homeward bound from Mars, and though they had been experiencing normal earth weight for the last weeks of their voyage—thanks to the spin of their liner—they obviously didn't like it yet. They walked very gingerly, and were always finding excuses to go "up" to the top floor, where gravity had the same value as on Mars.

I had never met any Martian colonists before, and they fascinated me. Their clothes, their accents—everything about them had an air of strangeness, though often it was hard to say just where the peculiarity lay. They all seemed to know each other by their first names. Perhaps that wasn't surprising after their long voyage, but later I discovered it was just the same on Mars. The settlements there were still small enough for everyone to know everybody else. They would find things very different when they got to earth.

I felt a little lonely among all these strangers, and it was some time before I made any acquaintances. There were some small shops on the "Two Thirds Gravity" deck, where one could buy toilet goods and souvenirs, and I was exploring these when three young colonists came strolling in. The oldest was a boy who looked about my age, and he was accompanied by two girls who were obviously his sisters.

"Hello," he said, "*you* weren't on the ship."

"No," I answered. "I've just come over from the other half of the station."

"What's your name?"

So blunt a request must have seemed rude or at least ill-mannered down on earth, but by now I learned that the colonists were like that. They were direct and forthright and never wasted words. I decided to behave in the same way.

"I'm Roy Malcolm. Who are you?"

"Oh," said one of the girls, "we read about you in the ship's newspaper. You've been flying round the moon, and all sorts of things."

I was quite flattered to find that they'd heard of me, but merely shrugged my shoulders as if it wasn't anything of importance. In any case, I didn't want to risk showing off, as they'd traveled a lot farther than I had.

"I'm John Moore," announced the boy, "and these are my sisters Ruby and May. This is the first time we've been to earth."

"You mean you were born on Mars?"

"That's right. We're coming home to go to college."

It sounded strange to hear that phrase "coming home" from someone who'd never set foot on earth. I nearly asked "Can't you get a good education on Mars, then?" but luckily stopped myself in time. The colonists were very sensitive to criticism of their planet, even when it wasn't intended. They also hated the word "colonist," and you had to avoid using it when they were around. But you couldn't very well call them "Martians," for that word had to be saved for the original inhabitants of the planet.

"We're looking for some souvenirs to take home," said Ruby. "Don't you think that plastic star map is beautiful?"

"I liked that carved meteor best," I said. "But it's an awful price."

"How much have you got?" said John.

I turned out my pockets and did a quick calculation. To my astonishment, John immediately replied, "I can lend you the rest. You can let me have it back when we reach earth."

This was my first contact with the quick-hearted generosity which everyone took for granted on Mars. I couldn't possibly accept the offer, yet didn't want to hurt John's feelings. Luckily I had a good excuse.

"That's fine of you," I said, "but I've just remembered that I've used up my weight allowance. So that settles it. I can't take home anything else."

I waited anxiously for a minute in case one of the Moores was willing to lend me cargo space as well, but fortunately they must all have used up their allowances too.

After this, it was inevitable that they took me to meet their parents. We found them in the main lounge, puzzling their way through the newspapers from earth. As soon as she saw me, Mrs. Moore exclaimed, "What *has* happened to your clothes!" and for the first time I realized that life on the Inner Station had made quite a mess of my suit. Before I knew what had happened, I'd been pushed into a brightly colored suit of John's. It was a good fit, but the design was startling, at least by earth standards, though it certainly wasn't noticeable here.

We all had so much to talk about that the hours spent waiting for the ferry passed extremely quickly. Life on Mars was as novel to me as life on earth was to the Moores. John had a fine collection of photographs which he'd taken, showing what it was like in the great pressure-domed cities and out on the colored deserts. He'd done quite a bit of traveling and had some wonderful pictures of Martian scenery and life. They were so good that I suggested he sell them to the illustrated magazines. He answered, in a slightly hurt voice, "I already have."

The photograph that fascinated me most was a view over one of the great vegetation areas—the Syrtis Major, John told me. It had been taken from a considerable height, looking down the slope of a wide valley. Millions of years ago the short-lived Martian seas had rolled above this land, and the bones of strange marine creatures were still embedded in its rocks. Now new life was returning to the planet. Down in the valley, great machines were turning up the brick-red soil to make way for the colonists from earth. In the distance I could see acres of the so-called "Air-weed," freshly planted in neat rows. As it grew, this strange plant would break down the minerals in the ground and release free oxygen, so that one day men would be able to live on the planet without breathing masks.

Mr. Moore was standing in the foreground, with a small Martian on either side of him. The little creatures were grasping his fingers with tiny, clawlike hands and staring at the camera with their huge, pale eyes. There was something rather touching about the scene. It seemed to dramatize the friendly contact of two races in a way that nothing else could do.

"Why," I exclaimed suddenly, "your dad isn't wearing a breathing mask!"

John laughed.

"I was wondering when you'd notice that. It'll be a long time before there's enough free oxygen in the atmosphere for us to breathe it, but some of us can manage without a mask for a couple of minutes—as long as we're not doing anything very energetic, that is."

"How do you get on with the Martians?" I asked. "Do you think they had a civilization once?"

"I don't know about that," said John. "Every so often you hear rumors of ruined cities out in the deserts, but they always turn out to be hoaxes or practical jokes. There's no evidence at all that the Martians were ever any different from what they are today. They're not exactly friendly, except when they're young, but they never give any trouble. The adults just ignore you unless you get in their way. They've got very little curiosity."

"I've read somewhere," I said, "that they behave more like rather intelligent horses than any other animal we've got on earth."

"I wouldn't know," said John. "I've never met a horse."

That brought me up with a jerk. Then I realized that there couldn't be many animals that John *had* met. Earth would have a great many surprises for him.

"Exactly what are you going to do when you get to earth?" I asked John. "Apart from going to college, that is."

"Oh, we'll travel round first and have a look at the sights. We've seen a lot of films, you know, so we've a good idea what it's like."

I did my best to avoid a smile. Though I'd lived in several countries, I hadn't really seen much of earth in my whole life, and I wondered if the Moores really realized just *how* big the planet was. Their scales of values must be quite different from mine. Mars is a small planet, and there are only limited regions where life is possible. If you put all the vegetation areas together, they wouldn't add up to much more than a medium-sized country down on earth. And, of course, the areas covered by the pressure-domes of the few cities are very much smaller still.

I decided to find out what my new friends really did know about earth.

"Surely," I said, "there are some places you particularly want to visit."

"Oh, yes!" replied Ruby. "*I* want to see some forests. Those great trees you have—we've nothing like them on Mars. It must be wonderful walking beneath their branches and seeing the birds flying around."

"We've got no birds either, you see," put in May rather wistfully. "The air's too thin for them."

"*I* want to see the ocean," said John. "I'd like to go sailing and fishing. It's true, isn't it, that you can get so far out to sea that you can't tell where the land is?"

"It certainly is," I replied.

Ruby gave a little shudder.

"All that water! It would scare me. I should be afraid of being lost—and I've read that being on a boat makes you horribly sick."

"Oh," I replied airily, "you get used to it. Of course,

there aren't many boats now, except for pleasure. A few hundred years ago most of the world's trade went by sea, until the air transport took over. You can hire boats at the coast resorts, though, and people who'll run them for you."

"But is it *safe?*" insisted Ruby. "I've read that your seas are full of horrible monsters that might come up and swallow you."

This time I couldn't help smiling.

"I shouldn't worry," I replied. "It hardly ever happens these days."

"What about the land animals?" asked May. "Some of those are quite big, aren't they? I've read about tigers and lions, and I *know* they're dangerous. I'm scared of meeting one of those."

Then I thought, I hope I know a bit more about Mars than you do about earth! I was just going to explain that man-eating tigers weren't generally found in our cities when I caught Ruby grinning at John, and realized that they'd been pulling my leg all the time.

After that we all went to lunch together, in a great dining room where I felt rather ill at ease. I made matters worse by forgetting we were under gravity again and spilling a glass of water on the floor. However, everyone laughed so good-humoredly I didn't really mind. The only person who was annoyed was the steward who had to mop it up.

For the rest of my short stay in the Residential Station I spent most of my time with the Moores. And it was here, surprisingly enough, that I at last saw something I'd missed on my other trips. Though I'd visited several space stations, I'd never actually watched one being built. We were now able to get a grandstand view of this operation —and without bothering to wear space suits. The Residential Station was being extended, and from the windows at the end of the "Two Thirds Gravity" floor we were able to see the whole fascinating process. Here was something that I could explain to my new friends. I didn't tell them

that the spectacle would have been equally strange to me
only two weeks ago.

The fact that we were making one complete revolution
every ten seconds was highly confusing at first, and the girls
turned rather green when they saw the stars orbiting outside the windows. However, the complete absence of vibration made it easy to pretend—just as one does on earth
—that *we* were stationary and it was really the stars that
were revolving.

The station extension was still a mass of open girders,
only partly covered by metal sheets. It had not yet been set
spinning, for that would have made its construction im-
possibly difficult. At the moment, it floated about half a
mile away from us, with a couple of freight rockets along-
side. When it was completed, it would be brought gently
up to the station and set rotating on its axis by small rocket
motors. As soon as the spins had been matched exactly,
the two units would be bolted together and the Residential
Station would have doubled its length. The whole operation
would be rather like engaging a gigantic clutch.

As we watched, a construction gang was easing a large
girder from the hold of a ferry rocket. The girder was about
forty feet long, and though it weighed nothing out here, its
mass or inertia was unchanged. It took a considerable effort
to start it moving, and an equal effort to stop it again. The
men of the construction crew were working in what were
really tiny spaceships, little cylinders about ten feet long,
fitted with low-powered rockets and steering jets. They
maneuvered these with fascinating skill, darting forward or
sideways and coming to rest with inches to spare. Ingenious handling mechanisms and jointed metal arms enabled them to carry out all ordinary assembling tasks almost as easily as if they were working with their own hands.

The team was under the radio control of a foreman—
or, to give him his more dignified name, a controller—who
stayed in a little pressure-hut fixed to the girders of the
partly constructed station. Moving to and fro or up and
down under his directions, and keeping in perfect unison,
they reminded me of a flock of goldfish in a pool. Indeed,

with sunlight glinting on their armor, they did look very much like underwater creatures.

The girder was now floating free of the ship that had brought it here from the moon, and two of the men attached their grapples and towed it slowly toward the station. Much too late, it seemed to me, they began to use their braking units. But there was still a good six inches between the girder and the skeleton framework when they had finished. Then one of the men went back to help his colleagues with the unloading, while the other eased the girder across the structure. It was not lying in exactly the correct line, so he had to slew it through a slight angle as well. Then he slipped in the bolts and began to tighten them up. It all looked so effortless, but I realized that immense skill and practice must lie behind this deceptive simplicity.

Before you could go down to earth, you were supposed to spend a twelve-hour quarantine period on the "Full Earth Gravity" floor—the outermost of the station's three decks. So once again I went down one of those curving stairways, my weight increasing with every step. When I had reached the bottom, my legs felt very weak and wobbly. I could hardly believe that *this* was the normal force of gravity under which I had passed my whole life.

The Moores had come with me, and they felt the strain even more than I did. This was three times the gravity of their native Mars, and twice I had to stop John from falling as he tottered unsteadily about. The third time I failed, and we both went down together. We looked so miserable that after a minute each started laughing at the other's expression and our spirits quickly revived. For a while we sat on the thick rubber flooring (the designers of the station had known where it would be needed!) and got up our strength for another attempt. This time we didn't fall down. Much to John's annoyance, the remainder of his family managed much better than he did.

We couldn't leave the Residential Station without seeing one of its prize exhibits. The "Full Earth Gravity" floor had a swimming pool, a small one, but its fame had spread throughout the solar system.

It was famous because it wasn't flat. As I've explained, since the station's "gravity" was caused by its spin, the vertical at any spot pointed toward the central axis. Any free water, therefore, had a concave surface, taking the shape of a hollow cylinder.

We couldn't resist entering the pool, not merely because once we were floating, gravity would be less of a strain. Though I'd become used to many strange things in space, it was a weird feeling to stand with my head just above the surface of the pool and to look along the water. In one direction, parallel to the axis of the station, the surface was quite flat. But in the other it was curved upward on either side of me. At the edge of the pool, in fact, the water level was higher than my head. I seemed to be floating in the trough of a great frozen wave. At any moment I expected the water to come flooding down as the surface flattened itself out. But it didn't, because it was already "flat" in this strange gravity field. (When I got back to earth I made quite a mess trying to demonstrate this effect by whirling a bucket of water round my head at the end of a string. If you try the same experiment, make sure you're out of doors!)

We could not play around in that peculiar pool as long as I would have liked, for presently the loud-speakers began to call softly and I knew that my time was running out. All the passengers were asked to check the packing of their luggage and to assemble in the main hall of the station. The colonists, I knew, were planning some kind of farewell, and though it didn't really concern me, I felt sufficiently interested to go along. After talking to the Moores I'd begun to like them and to understand their point of view a good deal better.

It was a subdued little gathering that we joined a few minutes later. These weren't tough, confident pioneers any more. They knew that soon they'd be separated and in a strange world, among millions of other human beings with totally different modes of life. All their talk about "going home" seemed to have evaporated; it was Mars, not earth, they were homesick for now.

As I listened to their farewells and little speeches, I suddenly felt very sorry for them. And I felt sorry for myself, because in a few hours I too would be saying good-by to space.

12 THE LONG FALL HOME

◆◆◆◆◆◆◆◆◆◆◆◆◆◆◆◆◆◆◆◆◆◆◆◆◆◆◆◆◆◆◆◆◆◆◆◆◆◆

I HAD come up from earth by myself, but I was going home in plenty of company. There were nearly fifty passengers crowded into the "One Third Gravity" floor waiting to disembark. That was the complement for the first rocket: the rest of the colonists would be going down on later flights.

Before we left the station, we were all handed a bundle of leaflets full of instructions, warnings and advice about conditions on earth. I felt that it was hardly necessary for me to read through all this, but was quite glad to have another souvenir of my visit. It was certainly a good idea giving these leaflets out at this stage in the homeward journey, because it kept most of the passengers so busy reading that they didn't have time to worry about anything else until we'd landed.

The air lock was only large enough to hold about a dozen people at a time, so it took quite a while to shepherd us all through. As each batch left the station, the lock had to be set revolving to counteract its normal spin, then it had to be coupled to the waiting spaceship, uncoupled again when the occupants had gone through, and the whole sequence restarted. I wondered what would happen if something jammed while the spinning station was connected to the stationary ship. Probably the ship would come off worse—that is, next to the unfortunate people in the air lock! However, I discovered later there was an additional movable coupling to take care of just such an emergency.

The earth ferry was the biggest spaceship I had ever been inside. There was one large cabin for the passengers, with rows of seats in which we were supposed to remain strapped during the trip. Since I was lucky enough to be one of the first to go aboard, I was able to get a seat near a window. Most of the passengers had nothing to look at but each other and the handful of leaflets they'd been given to read.

We waited for nearly an hour before everyone was aboard and the luggage had been stowed away. Then the loud-speakers told us to stand by for take-off in five minutes. The ship had now been completely uncoupled from the station and had drifted several hundred feet away from it.

I had always thought that the return to earth would be rather an anticlimax after the excitement of a take-off. There was a different sort of feeling, it was true, but it was still quite an experience. Until now we had been, if not beyond the power of gravity, at least traveling so swiftly in our orbit that earth could never pull us down. But now we were going to throw away the speed that gave us safety. We would descend until we had re-entered the atmosphere and were forced to spiral back to the surface. If we came in too steeply, our ship might blaze across the sky like a meteor and come to the same fiery end.

I looked at the tense faces around me. Perhaps the Martian colonists were thinking the same thoughts. Perhaps they were wondering what they were going to meet and do down on the planet which so few of them had ever before seen. I hoped that none of them would be disappointed.

Three sharp notes from the loud-speaker gave us the last warning. Five seconds later the motors opened up gently, quickly increasing power to full thrust. I saw the Residential Station fall swiftly astern, its great, spinning drum dwindling against the stars. Then, with a lump in my throat, I watched the untidy maze of girders and pressure chambers that housed so many of my friends go swimming by. Useless though the gesture was, I couldn't help giving them a wave. After all, they knew I was aboard this ship and might catch a glimpse of me through the window.

Now the two components of the Inner Station were receding rapidly behind us and soon had passed out of sight under the great wing of the ferry. It was hard to realize that in reality *we* were losing speed while the station continued on its unvarying way. And as we lost speed, so we would start falling down to earth on a long curve that would take us to the other side of the planet before we entered the atmosphere.

After a surprisingly short period, the motors cut out again. We had shed all the speed that was necessary, and gravity would do the rest. Most of the passengers had settled down to read, but I decided to have my last look at the stars, undimmed by atmosphere. This was also my last chance of experiencing weightlessness, but it was wasted because I couldn't leave my seat. I did try—and got shooed back by the steward.

The ship was now pointing *against* the direction of its orbital motion and had to be swung round so that it entered the atmosphere nose first. There was plenty of time to carry out this maneuver, and the pilot did it in a leisurely fashion with the low-powered steering jets at the wing-tips. From where I was sitting I could see the short columns of mist stabbing from the nozzles, and very slowly the stars swung around us. It was a full ten minutes before we came to rest again, with the nose of the ship now pointing due east.

We were still almost five hundred miles above the Equator, moving at nearly eighteen thousand miles an hour. But we were now slowly dropping earthward. In thirty minutes we would make our first contact with the atmosphere.

John was sitting next to me, and so I had a chance of airing my knowledge of geography.

"That's the Pacific Ocean down there," I said. And something prompted me to add, not very tactfully, "You could drop Mars in it without going near either of the coast lines."

However, John was too fascinated by the great expanse of water to take any offense. It must have been an overwhelming sight for anyone who had lived on sealess Mars. There are not even any permanent lakes on that planet, only a few shallow pools that form around the melting icecaps in the summer. And now John was looking down upon water that stretched as far as he could see in every direction, with a few specks of land dotted upon it here and there.

"Look," I said, "there, straight ahead! You can see the coast line of South America. We can't be more than two hundred miles up now."

Still in utter silence, the ship dropped earthward and the ocean rolled back beneath us. No one was reading now if he had a chance of seeing from one of the windows. I felt very sorry for the passengers in the middle of the cabin who weren't able to watch the approaching landscape beneath.

The coast of South America flashed by in seconds, and ahead lay the great jungles of the Amazon. *Here* was life on a scale that Mars could not match, not even, perhaps, in the days of its youth. Thousands of square miles of crowded forests, countless streams and rivers were unfolding beneath us, so swiftly that as soon as one feature had been grasped, it was already out of sight.

Now the great river was widening as we shot above its course. We were approaching the Atlantic, which should have been visible by this time, but which seemed to be hidden by mists. As we passed above the mouth of the Amazon, I saw that a great storm was raging below. From time to time brilliant flashes of lightning played across the clouds. It was uncanny to see all this happening in utter silence as we raced high overhead.

"A tropical storm," I said to John. "Do you ever have anything like that on Mars?"

"Not with rain, of course," he said. "But sometimes we get pretty bad sandstorms over the deserts. And I've seen lightning once or perhaps twice."

"What, without rain clouds?" I asked.

"Oh, yes, the sand gets electrified. Not very often, but it *does* happen."

The storm was now far behind us, and the Atlantic lay smooth in the evening sun. We would not see it much longer, however, for darkness lay ahead. We were nearing the night side of the planet, and on the horizon I could see a band of shadow swiftly approaching as we hurtled into twilight. There was something terrifying about plunging headlong into that curtain of darkness. In mid-Atlantic we lost the sun, and at almost the same moment we heard the first whisper of air along the hull.

It was an eerie sound, and it made the hair rise at the back of my neck. After the silence of space any noise seemed wrong. But it grew steadily as the minutes passed, from a faint, distant wail to a high-pitched scream. We were still more than fifty miles up, but at the speed we were traveling even the incredibly thin atmosphere of these heights was protesting as we tore through it.

More than that, it was tearing at the ship, slowing it down. There was a faint but steadily increasing tug from our straps; the deceleration was trying to force us out of our seats. It was like sitting in a car when the brakes are being slowly applied. But in this case, the braking was going to last for two hours, and we would go once more round the world before we slowed to a halt.

We were no longer in a spaceship but an airplane. In almost complete darkness—there was no moon—we passed above Africa and the Indian Ocean. The fact that we were speeding through the night, traveling above the invisible earth at many thousands of miles an hour, made it all the more impressive. The thin shriek of the upper atmosphere had become a steady background to our flight; it grew neither louder nor fainter as the minutes passed.

I was looking out into the darkness when I saw a faint red glow beneath me. At first, because there was no sense of perspective or distance, it seemed at an immense depth below the ship, and I could not imagine what it might be. A great forest fire, perhaps—but we were now, surely, over the ocean again. Then I realized, with a shock that nearly jolted me out of my seat, that this ominous red glow came from our wing. The heat of our passage through the atmosphere was turning it cherry-red.

I stared at that disturbing sight for several seconds before I decided that everything was really quite in order. All our tremendous energy of motion was being converted into heat, though I had never realized just how *much* heat would be produced. For the glow was increasing even as I watched. When I flattened my face against the window, I could see part of the leading edge, and it was a bright yellow in places. I wondered if the other passengers had noticed it, or perhaps the little leaflets, which I hadn't bothered to read, had already told them not to worry.

I was glad when we emerged into daylight once more, greeting the dawn above the Pacific. The glow from the wings was no longer visible, and so ceased to worry me. Besides, the sheer splendor of the sunrise, which we were approaching at nearly ten thousand miles an hour, took away all other sensations. From the Inner Station, I had watched many dawns and sunsets pass across the earth. But up there I had been detached, not part of the scene itself. Now I was once more inside the atmosphere and these wonderful colors were all around me.

We had now made one complete circuit of the earth and had shed more than half our speed. It was much longer, this time, before the Brazilian jungles came into view, and they passed more slowly now. Above the mouth of the Amazon the storm was still raging, only a little way beneath us, as we started out on our last crossing of the South Atlantic.

Then night came once more, and there again was the wing glowing redly in the darkness around the ship. It seemed even hotter now, but perhaps I had grown used to it, for the sight no longer worried me. We were nearly home, on the last lap of the journey. By now we must have lost so much speed that we were probably traveling no faster than many normal aircraft.

A cluster of lights along the coast of East Africa told us that we were heading out over the Indian Ocean again. I wished I could be up in the control cabin, watching the preparations for the final approach to the spaceport. By now the pilot would have picked up the guiding radio beacons and would be coming down the beam, still at a great speed but according to a carefully prearranged program. When we reached New Guinea, our velocity would be almost completely spent. Our ship would be nothing more than a great glider, flying through the night sky on the last dregs of its momentum.

The loud-speaker broke into my thoughts.

"Pilot to passengers. We shall be landing in twenty minutes."

Even without this warning, I could tell that the flight was nearing its end. The scream of the wind outside our hull had dropped in pitch, and there had been a perceptible change of direction as the ship slanted downward. And, most striking sign of all, the red glow outside the window was rapidly fading. Presently there were only a few dull patches left, near the leading edge of the wing. A few minutes later, even these had gone.

It was still night as we passed over Sumatra and Borneo. From time to time the lights of ships and cities winked into view and went astern—very slowly now, it seemed, after the headlong rush of our first circuit. At frequent intervals the loud-speaker called out our speed and position. We were traveling at less than a thousand miles an hour when we passed over the deeper darkness that was the New Guinea coast line.

"There it is!" I whispered to John. The ship had banked slightly, and beneath the wing was a great constellation of lights. A signal flare rose up in a slow, graceful arc and exploded into crimson fire. In the momentary glare, I caught a glimpse of the white mountain peaks surrounding the spaceport, and I wondered just how much margin of height we had. It would be very ironic to meet with disaster in the last few miles after traveling all this distance.

I never knew the actual moment when we touched down, the landing was so perfect. At one instant we were still air-borne, at the next the lights of the runway were rolling past as the ship slowly came to rest. I sat quite still in my seat, trying to realize that I was back on earth again. Then I looked at John. Judging from his expression, he could hardly believe it either.

The steward came around to help people release their seat straps and give last-minute advice. As I looked at the slightly harassed visitors, I could not help a mild feeling of superiority. I knew my way about on earth, but all this must be very strange to them. They must be realizing, also, that they were now in the full grip of earth's gravity, and there was nothing they could do about it until they were out in space again.

As we had been the first to enter the ship, we were the last to leave it. I helped John with some of his personal luggage, as he was obviously not very happy and wanted at least one hand free to grab any convenient support.

"Cheer up!" I said. "You'll soon be jumping around just as much as you did on Mars!"

"I hope you're right," he answered gloomily. "At the moment I feel like a cripple who's lost his crutch."

Mr. and Mrs. Moore, I noticed, had expressions of grim determination on their faces as they walked cautiously to the air lock. But if they wished they were back on Mars, they kept their feelings to themselves. So did the girls, who for some reason seemed less worried by gravity than any of us.

We emerged under the shadow of the great wing, the thin mountain air blowing against our faces. It was quite warm, surprisingly so, in fact, for night at such a high altitude. Then I realized that the wing above us was still hot—

probably too hot to touch, even though it was no longer visibly glowing.

We moved slowly away from the ship toward the waiting transport vehicles. Before I stepped into the bus that would take us across to the Port buildings. I looked up once more at the starlit sky that had been my home for a little while, and which, I was resolved, would be my home again. Up there in the shadow of the earth, speeding the traffic that moved from world to world, were Commander Doyle, Tim Benton, Ronnie Jordan, Norman Powell, and all the other friends I'd made on my visit to the Inner Station. I remembered Commander Doyle's promise, and wondered how soon I would remind him of it. . . .

John Moore was waiting patiently behind me, clutching the door handle of the bus. He saw me looking up into the sky and followed my gaze.

"You won't be able to see the station," I said. "It's in eclipse."

John didn't answer, and then I saw that he was staring into the east, where the first hint of dawn glowed along the horizon. High against these unfamiliar southern stars was something that I did recognize, a brilliant, ruby beacon, the brightest object in the sky.

"My home," said John, in a faint, sad voice.

I stared into that beckoning light and remembered the pictures John had shown me and the stories he had told. Up there were the great colored deserts, the old sea-beds that man was bringing once more to life, the little Martians who might, or might not, belong to a race that was more ancient than ours.

And I knew that, after all, I was going to disappoint Commander Doyle. The space stations were too near home to satisfy me now. My imagination had been captured by that little red world glowing bravely against the stars. When I went into space again, the Inner Station would only be the first milestone on my outward road from earth.

Ø

Other SIGNET Science Fiction Titles You Will Enjoy

Other SIGNET Science Fiction
You Will Want to Read

THE NEW AMERICAN LIBRARY, INC.,
P.O. Box 999, Bergenfield, New Jersey 07621

Please send me the SIGNET BOOKS I have checked above. I am enclosing $_____(check or money order—no currency or C.O.D.'s). Please include the list price plus 25¢ a copy to cover handling and mailing costs. (Prices and numbers are subject to change without notice.)

Name_____

Address_____

City_____State_____Zip Code_____
Allow at least 3 weeks for delivery